MURDER TOWN

"I had to hog-tie you, seein's how you went at us before," a voice said. "Name's Jared Cable. I'm a black-smith. Town marshal, too."

The tied man stared at his bonds. "Cut these ropes."

"Can't. Until I know you're going to stay calm, I can't cut you loose."

"Why am I being treated like a criminal?"

"Because there's been two murders here in the valley this past week. First in its history. Folks are scared. I might as well ask you: Why were those riders gunning after you?"

"It's my business, not yours."

"You ain't cooperating, friend."

The prisoner glared. "I came here just to be coming. No reason. That's the truth. My name's Tellico. Now cut these ropes and I'll ride out again."

"I'm afraid you won't," Jared said. "This town is snowed in." Jared produced a knife and began sawing at Tellico's ropes.

Tellico stood, rubbing his wrists. He went to the window. Hard snow pelted against the pane. He laughed ironically. "Snowed in . . . in a murder town."

JERUSALEM CAMP

Cameron Judd

BANTAM BOOKS

NEW YORK · TORONTO · LONDON · SYDNEY · AUCKLAND

JERUSALEM CAMP

A Bantam Book / July 1989

ISBN 0-553-28149-6

Published simultaneously in the United States and Canada

Bantam Books are published by Bantam Books, a division of Bantam
Doubleday Dell Publishing Group, Inc. Its trademark, consisting of
the words "Bantam Books" and the portrayal of a rooster, is Reg-
istered in U.S. Patent and Trademark Office and in other countries.
Marca Registrada, Bantam Books, 666 Fifth Avenue, New York, New
York 10103.

PRINTED IN THE UNITED STATES OF AMERICA

O   0 9 8 7 6 5 4 3 2 1

JERUSALEM CAMP

Chapter 1

He came to the mountains as the snow fell, and the clip of his big bay's hooves marked off the changing of the seasons. Later, the people of Jerusalem Camp would recall his time among them as the Killing Winter. The man himself they would recall only by the single name he gave them, for he never gave another, and when at last he rode out again with a new season at his heels, he rode out for good.

He climbed the Sierras with a bullet crease in his leg and the two armed riders who had put it there close behind him. He pushed the bay along canyon flanks, beneath granite cliffs, and up washes lined with tamarack and sugar pine. Gray clouds spat snow that piled thickly on the ground and hampered the bay. The rider looked back frequently, and bent low, perhaps from pain, perhaps just to make himself less conspicuous.

He slowed when he reached a snow-encrusted stand of pine that was so closely bunched his horse could barely push through. When at last it did and then ascended a slope, the rider looked back and saw his pursuers already coming through the stand. Too close. He spurred his horse, but the weary animal, sides heaving and nostrils spewing steam, could go no faster.

On a jumble of talus at the base of a black escarpment, the bay stepped into a hole and pitched, whinnying, to the left. As the rider fell painfully on rock shards, he heard the snap of the horse's left foreleg.

He rose and wiped blood from his shattered lip onto his sleeve. He glanced once into the tormented eyes of his fallen horse and vainly wished he had the time and spare ammunition to end the beast's suffering.

In the cold air a shot from behind him made a flat, slapping sound that echoed off the escarpment. He struggled forward, came to a ravine, and leapt into it. He pulled icy air into his lungs; it burned like cold fire.

He looked at his wounded leg: still bleeding. At least it didn't hurt. The strain and the cold had numbed him so he did not feel it, the snow beneath his thin boot soles, or the slice of the wind through his canvas trousers.

He scrambled along the ravine, but his progress was too slow. So, gritting his teeth, he rolled up out of it on his back and belly. He stood and was surprised to see four men before him. Strangers, armed. They had just emerged from a scraggly forest of pine a hundred feet ahead.

Another shot sounded behind him; the bullet zipped over his head. One of the strangers ahead raised a rifle and fired back. The lone man was caught in the middle.

He dropped back into the ravine, his face digging into the snow. He heard more gunfire back and forth, then suddenly it stopped. For several seconds, the Sierras were utterly silent. The man cautiously stood and peered over the edge of the ravine. The four from the forest approached, rifles smoking. He glanced behind; his pursuers were gone.

He smiled as the four men reached him, and said, "I'm obliged—" but one of the men drew back his rifle, brought down the butt, and knocked him cold.

The four men gathered around the edge of the ravine

and looked at his still form, silent as their breath made white fog in the mountain air and fear they dared not reveal tasted like bile in their throats.

Jared learned of the capture from Jimmy Essler, a boy who lived several houses up from his forge. The gap-toothed boy was very excited and lisped it out to the blacksmith like this: "Mither Cable, they got a man caught and down at Mither Rupert and Mither Rupert ith ready to hang him!"

"What? Hang who?"

"The man! They caught the man!"

Jared saw that he would gain no understanding from Jimmy, so he hurriedly dusted off his hands, doffed his leather smith's apron, and slipped on his coat. The smithy was hot, but outside the snow churned down in a near-blizzard and the twilight air was biting cold.

Jimmy came out at Jared's heels and passed him at a dead run through the contorted field of white. The flakes fell so thickly that before Jimmy was twenty feet ahead Jared lost sight of him.

Rupert's was a store in one way of looking at it, and a saloon and gambling house in another. Loren Rupert was dedicated to keeping vice alive in Jerusalem Camp, a purpose that had set him firmly against Jared Cable's preacher father ever since Rupert had drifted up from the American River camps years ago. Now that Jared had accepted the mostly symbolic job of town marshal, he suspected that he was replacing his aging father as Rupert's chief object of wrath.

Rupert's door tended to jam, then pop open loudly, so when Jared entered he got the full attention of every man inside. It was a solemn gathering: Rupert and four no-goods who hung around his place. Jimmy Essler was there, too, having scrambled in ahead of Jared. Jared smelled the familiar mix of hot coffee, woodsmoke, chalk dust, and whiskey that permeated the building.

Rupert, his gray and black hair slick with bay rum, said with thick, smiling sarcasm, "Well, look here, boys. It's the marshal."

"Hello, Loren," Jared said. He looked down at Jimmy, whose red hair was growing damp as the snow flecked on it melted in the heat of Rupert's pine-fed stove. "Boy, you'd best get on before your ma worries."

"Aw, c'mon, Mither Cable," the boy complained. "Anytime anything geth tharted I get thent off."

"Get on," Jared repeated.

The boy's face darkened, but immediately brightened. "I know what I'll do," he said. He opened the door and vanished as before into the white swirl.

Jared said, "The boy mentioned something about a man, and a hanging—"

Clyde Ingersoll, whose bulbous nose might have been red from cold but more likely from something else, said, "This ain't your business, Cable."

"You got a man here or not?" Jared demanded. Rupert gave an almost mischievous grin. "We do."

"Where?"

Rupert thumbed toward a storage room behind him.

Jared entered. The rider lay on the bare floor. He had been unconscious, but was starting to rouse.

"Who is he?" Jared asked.

"How should I know?" Rupert said. "We caught him coming in toward town with two men shooting at him. We took it they might be shooting at us, too, and shot back. He's the one we're after—that I'll wager."

"Now how do you know that?"

"Who else could he be?"

Jared shook his head. "You never fail to astound me,

Rupert. Not a shred of evidence and you're ready to string up a man just because he rode through at the wrong time." Jared paused when he saw the blood on the man's trousers. "You've shot him!"

"He was shot before we ever seen him," Rupert said defensively. "It's just a crease. And nobody's said nothing about stringing him up. That was just the boy talking."

"I'll bet."

Jared briefly searched the man's pockets, looking for identification. He found nothing, but he noted a leather string around the man's neck, extending below his shirt. Jared pulled it out. On it hung an oval brass medallion, worn nearly smooth so its image of a tree and a river was now only scarcely visible.

"What's that?" Rupert asked. Jared shook his head.

Behind them the balky door popped open again and Logan Hull entered. Doc Hull, the townsfolk called him, though his medical credentials didn't strictly justify it. He had worked in field hospitals during the war with Mexico—an effective school of medicine, but one that issued no diplomas or shingles to swing above doors.

Doc Hull walked into the back room and knelt beside the supine man, whose eyes fluttered open a second later. The others regrouped around him. The man looked around the room, resting his gaze for a moment on each face. Doc said, "Easy, my friend. I'm a doctor. Let me check you."

"How'd you hear about this, Doc?" Jared asked.

"Jimmy Essler just now told me. I sent him home."

Hull prodded the furrowed bullet wound. The man winced.

"Sorry, son," Doc said. "I'm just checking on—"

With speed that surprised them all, the man burst upward. He pushed back Hull, who fell on his rump. A fast swing brought down Ingersoll, and the follow-through hammered Rupert's jaw with a sound like a cracking walnut. The store owner staggered, flailed out for a handhold, and grabbed the hot pipe of his woodstove. He screeched, let go, and fell atop Ingersoll.

Rupert's other cronies yelled and leapt away. Wild-eyed, the stranger brought back his fist and charged at Jared.

The man was fast, but Jared, spurred by surprise, was faster. He rolled up a fist big as a muskmelon and drove it bullet-straight into the stranger's mouth. The man's legs went soft, and he fell to his knees, teetered for a second with his arms limp at his sides, then pitched facedown onto the floor, once again out cold.

Two men stood shivering in the snow-whipped mountain wilderness. One said, "We're lost. Sooner we admit it and get to town, the better."

"A group from that town shot at us, Joe. It wouldn't be sensible."

"Is it sensible to freeze to death?"

The other had no answer. All about them snow blotted the horizon, making every direction the same. Finally, the one named Joe said what both had been unwillingly thinking: "We'll be like the Donner party if we don't get to shelter. Maybe we should go back to the cabin with Frank."

Mansell looked around at the deathly white. His horse stamped and pawed in the snow. "Forget about Frank," he said. "We'd never find the way there anyway. We'll try for the town. It lies yonder."

The other frowned. "I thought it was that way—"

"Yonder," Mansell said emphatically. But he wasn't as sure as he sounded.

They plunged forward, leading their mounts, stepping high in the rising drifts. The effort was three times harder than it would have been on bare ground, and their hearts hammered at their ribs. Joe screwed his hat low in a vain effort to shield ears so cold he couldn't even tell without feeling for them that they were still there. As they moved, terribly slowly, the day waned. Night slid over the sky like thick gray paint.

"We're going to die out here," Joe said.

"Shut up."

After fifteen minutes, neither could tell how far they had gone, nor if they had traveled straight or merely circled. Nor in which direction lay Jerusalem Camp. They plodded on as the snow piled to their knees.

At last they reached a clearing, now just a wide expanse of drifting snow. Without trees to filter and divert it, the snow had piled deeper here. It reached to the middle of their thighs; walking through it was like wading in half-frozen molasses.

Halfway across, they stopped. They had seen someone. A gray man who so blended with the murky, motile background that only with concentration could they distinguish his silhouette against it. He carried a Henry repeater and wore a heavy fur cloak that was colorless in the gloom.

Mansell felt a warm burst of relief. "Hello!" he called. He waved his arm above his head. "Can you help us!"

The figure stood unmoving, as silent as the snow that nearly hid him.

"Hello!" Mansell called again. "How far are we from Jerusalem Camp?"

There was a long silence. Then a deep voice said, "Near."

"Praise be. Which way?"

Another long pause, then, "You pilgrims lost?"

Some fast-rising instinct kept Mansell from answering. But his partner said, "Yes. Bad lost. Which way?"

The figure edged forward two steps. They could see his outline a bit more clearly now, but the dashing flakes blurred the details of his face. Only his wind-whipped beard, long and gray, was clearly visible. "Bad place for men to be lost," he said.

"Which way to Jerusalem Camp?" repeated Mansell, fighting a peculiar urge to back away.

The man waved to his right. "Beyond that rise."

"Thank you." They pulled their horses southward a few yards. Joe stopped and turned. The Gray Man remained as before.

"Are you going there, too?"

He didn't answer or move.

Mansell said, "You could freeze out here."

"I won't freeze. I can warm myself any moment in the fires of hell."

Mansell, amazed at the singular comment, wondered if the man was insane. But it was nearly dark; urgency compelled him to move. He and Joe struggled to the rise and looked across in the remaining feeble light. They saw no town. Nothing but wild, snowbound wilderness fading into gray nonentity.

"What the . . ." Mansell muttered. He turned. The Gray Man had followed them, but remained several yards behind. "Are you sure this is the way?"

"You will reach the town," the man said. "That I promise."

"But there's nothing there."

"I will send you to the town. I know it well. It is only just now beginning to know me."

Mansell looked at the sky. It was the color of slate

and growing darker. A burst of panic constricted his throat.

"Who are you?"

The old man smiled and came toward him. "Who are you?" Mansell demanded again, backing away, cold hands vainly fumbling for his weapons as the old man, still smiling, bore down upon them with the Henry upraised.

Chapter 2

Ceaselessly the snow fell from clouds that blocked the stars and moon and made the night black as a cavern. As the people of Jerusalem Camp huddled by their fires, sheets of white covered the mountain passes. Heaps of snow piled thickly on evergreen branches, making them strain, then break. Massive limbs crashed earthward, across narrow paths and wagon roads that would accommodate no travelers from now until spring. High on the notch-shaped pass that was the only route out of the basin in which Jerusalem Camp lay, the snow lay especially deep, as it did there every winter, blocking the trail and turning the pass into a natural trap where avalanches were easily triggered.

The stranger slid for the second time into sluggish awareness. He lay in semidarkness, hurting all over. Tough rope bound his wrists and ankles. He was cold and very confused.

"I had to tie you up, what with how you went at us before," a voice said. "My name's Jared Cable. I'm a blacksmith. Town marshal, too." The speaker's face came into focus. Smiling but stern, it was the face of a strong man. One the stranger had seen when he had come to the first time.

The tied man strained at his bonds. "Cut these ropes."

"I can't. I don't blame you for flying off like you did, the way Rupert and his gang knocked you out. But until I know you're going to stay calm, I can't cut you loose."

"Why am I being treated like a criminal?"

"Because there's been two murders in this valley this past week. First in its history. Everybody's scared. Maybe that didn't give nobody the right to jump you, but jump you they did. And I might as well ask you, why were those riders gunning after you?"

"I owe you no explanations."

"No. But if you don't talk, you'll spend the rest of the winter tied in that bed."

The stranger exhaled slowly, frowning. Finally he said, "They were trying to rob me, I think. Followed me in from the foothills. You going to cut me loose now?"

"I might. What brought you to Jerusalem Camp?"

"My business, not yours."

"What's your name?"

"Not your business either."

Jared scratched his day-old beard. "All right. Suit yourself." He turned toward the door.

"You're leaving me like this?"

"You ain't cooperating, friend."

The prisoner glared bitterly at him. Finally he said, "I came here just to be coming. No reason. That's the truth. My name's Tellico."

"Tellico who?"

"Tellico's sufficient."

"So, Tellico's sufficient, you rode in to the mountains at the front end of a blizzard—for no reason?"

"That's right. Now cut these ropes and I'll ride out again."

"I'm afraid you won't," Jared said. "This town is snowed in. Funny thing about the lay of our land: The valley's like a bottle, with the pass being the spout. Once

snow corks it, you don't get out again." Jared produced
a knife and began sawing at Tellico's ropes.

"What's this about murder?"

"Two so far. Man name of Davison and his boy, both
out in the mountains when it happened. You picked a
bad time to ride in to Jerusalem Camp."

Tellico stood with difficulty, rubbing his wrists. He
went to a window and threw back the burlap curtain.
Snow pelted the pane, flakes frozen so hard they rattled
the glass. He laughed ironically. "Snowed in, in a murder
town."

"That's the size of it," Jared said.

Tellico turned and gave Jared his best chance yet
to view him. His hair was sandy, slightly long and rather
unruly. His eyes were an intense green. His skin was
ruddy and fair, though a heavy undergrowth of whiskers
somewhat darkened his cheeks. He was slender but far
from frail, and seemed tense as a fiddle string.

His shirt was blue, his trousers made of heavy,
slightly greasy canvas, his boots well worn and devoid
of ornamentation. When they had captured him he had
been wearing a gun belt with a Remington tucked into
it. Rupert had taken it, but Jared had reconfiscated it
from him.

"Am I a prisoner?" Tellico asked.

"Only of snow and circumstances. I've got no reason
to hold you, as long as you keep yourself out of trouble."

"All right."

"What are you going to do with yourself? You got
any means of support?"

The question, strangely, made Tellico laugh. "I've
been asking myself that very question for some time
now," he said. "But I'll survive. If I get hungry I can
hunt."

"You're taking being trapped here mighty well. Especially given the circumstances. There are those who won't think it a coincidence that you came in at the same time two people got murdered."

"I'll be careful."

"I won't lie to you, Tellico. I'll be watching you myself. I find you a believable man, somehow. But I can't believe any man rides into a wilderness like this, at a time like this, for no reason."

From the perspective of the hawks that circled above the white mountains, Jerusalem Camp was a nondescript, smoke-belching scattering of lumber squeezed between the granite mountainsides. It lay high above the foothills that were the more typical domain of California gold grubbers.

If it was an unusual town, that was appropriate, for it was populated by unusual people.

Three decades before, thousands of forty-niners had swarmed into California, panning the streams—and building flumes and races where there were no streams—erecting towns of canvas and wood along the rivers and tributaries, then quickly abandoning them when the gold ran out.

Amid this explosion of foothills activity a rumor arose: A gold-lined lake, people said, was hidden somewhere high in the mountains. Chunks of wealth just lying there to be picked up. An incredible story, but widely believed. So men scoured the mountains, looking for the lake and never finding it. But gold they did find here and there, and at those places they established camps. Jerusalem Camp was among them.

The Jerusalem Camp strike wasn't huge, but proved steady, so the camp lasted when many others did not, although it was an isolated settlement. It was seldom visited, except by the freighters who hauled in supplies enough to last the town through its isolated winters, and by occasional hunters and mountaineers.

On the edge of Jerusalem Camp stood a church. It was much more finely crafted than any of the town's other structures, with a steeple, bell, and arched double door-ways made of oak slabs and hung with brass. Except for miners' crude shacks, it was the first building in the camp.

That was fitting, for the men who had founded the church—the elders, people called them—also had founded the town. They had led the men of their con-gregation from Indiana across to the Sierras to establish a mountain utopia where civil, church, and work life would merge into one blissful existence. They named it New Jerusalem, but the name was quickly corrupted to Jerusalem Camp. That, to the dismay of the elders, proved symbolic of certain other corruptions to come.

But not at once. For a year and three months Je-rusalem Camp remained a religious community of labor under the control of the church. The saloons, whore-houses, bear-and-bull pits, and gambling halls that dom-inated other camps did not arise here. Jerusalem Camp's sanctified atmosphere was inhospitable to vice, choking it like a brine-doused weed.

Proud of their new town, a selected delegation of churchmen at last traveled east to fetch the families left behind. But when they arrived back in their utopia it had changed. That was chiefly because of Loren Rupert, who had come by way of the American River with a gambling wheel, several cases of whiskey, and a gaggle of decidedly unregenerate friends. All the opposition of the town's founding elders, led by the Reverend Isaiah Cable, could not drive him away. Jerusalem Camp lost its innocence. The church's exclusivity of influence was gone. The Reverend Isaiah Cable stood before his congregation and declared that now he knew firsthand what it was to see Eden fall. Then he leaned across his pulpit and cried. In the congregation his young son, Jared, newly arrived from Indiana, cried too. He had never seen his father weep, and it scared him.

It surprised no one that Loren Rupert and Isaiah Cable became foes. Isaiah preached against Rupert, and prayed from the pulpit for the damnation of his trade and the salvation of his soul. Rupert ridiculed him in return, and so it went on for years. Eventually, the people accepted the antagonism as a fixture of Jerusalem Camp, like its muddy, haphazard streets. Eventually, for lack of other options, the saints and sinners learned to live together, both sides reluctant and suspicious, but each affecting the other more than they would admit.

Jimmy Essler became suddenly and totally awake. His heart pounded rapidly; he felt a tingle of cognition that made him rise from his bed and slip to the window. Cold air poured in around the loose panes of glass, upon which snow piled in upward-slanting triangles against the crossbars.

The boy squinted through the darkness.

Nothing but deep night and swirling flakes. But he listened and heard the faint whinny of a horse.

Silently he darted through the little house, his footfalls softened by heavy woolen socks. His father snored in an adjacent room as Jimmy's mother stirred beside him, then settled again into the warmth of the rustling bed tick. Jimmy went to the front door and flung it open.

Snow spiraled into the house and stung his face. He diverted it from his eyes, with a hand laid knuckles-first against his forehead, and looked across the street. There was little light, but enough. Since the murders, some lamps in Jerusalem Camp were kept burning all night.

Jimmy looked at one of the lighted windows, and something dark passed across it.

His eyes grew wide and he became frightened. He closed the door. In a far corner of the house a mouse scratched for crumbs. The wind sang around the eaves and sent another blast of cold under the door.

His mother came to her bedroom door. "Jimmy?"

The boy looked at her. "Ith happened again, Ma."

"What are you talking about? Why are you out of bed?"

"Ith happened again. There'th dead men out there."

The woman stood silent a moment.

"Witt," she called to her husband. His snores became sputters, then he was awake. "Jimmy says there's dead men outside," she said.

Witt Essler rose and dressed. He took his rifle and went out.

In the center of the street stood two horses, shuddering in the cold. Two men sat astride them, straight and still, and despite the cold they did not shiver, and no steaming breath escaped them.

Witt raised his rifle and immediately wondered why he did so, for these men could be a threat to no one.

Whoever had lashed them to the horses had done a good job of it, even bothering to set poles to hold them erect. The right hands of both corpses were tied to their chests, making them appear to be vainly feeling for their own heartbeats. The right thumbs of both men were gone. Cut off just like those of the two Davisons when they were murdered.

Witt turned his face to the sky and shouted as loud as he could.

Chapter 3

Jared stood in the doorway of his smithy and watched the populace of Jerusalem Camp pass on the street. These were people he had known all his life, but they were afraid and their fear made them like strangers.

Two bodies strapped on boards leaned against the wall, awaiting an investigation by Doc Hull. From the expressions on their faces, these men had been very scared when they died. Fear was everywhere Jared looked.

He shivered. The wind stung his face like a slapping hand. The stock of his shotgun was cold and unfamiliar in his grip. He wasn't accustomed to carrying a firearm in town. Being the law in Jerusalem Camp wasn't supposed to have been a serious enterprise—or so the town fathers said when they hired him. That they had named a town marshal at all had been mostly for propriety's sake. A proper town had to have a marshal, they reasoned, even if few people broke the even fewer laws.

"But I don't want to be a town marshal," he had protested when Doc Hull told him of the decision. "I don't know nothing about the law business."

"Nothing to know," Doc had said. "You wear a badge if you want, and make sure Loren Rupert and his friends don't get too rowdy, and that's about it."

"What if something really bad happens?" Jared had asked.

Doc had laughed. "Nothing really bad ever happens in Jerusalem Camp."

The snow had diminished in the early morning, and now only sparse flakes danced on the brunt of the breeze to settle on the previous accumulation. Jared shifted his chilled frame within his heavy leather coat.

The people watched him subtly as they passed, flashing sidewise glances. Most remained silent. A handful actually approached the door, wanting to gawk at the bodies. Jared shook his head and waved them away.

At last Doc Hull came down the street, slightly bent as usual and puffing white steam through his whiskers. To his displeasure, Jared saw Rupert and Ingersoll approaching behind Doc with a handful of others. Jared scowled. Hang the human race; why do folks treat death like some kind of show?

"Howdy, Doc," Jared said sullenly, eyeing the others. "Come on inside."

Rupert started to walk inside as well. "Hold on," Jared said. "This ain't a circus."

Doc said, "Let them in, Jared. What's the difference?" So Jared shrugged and let them pass.

Doc knelt, winced arthritically, and studied the bodies. He pulled back the shirts and exposed the ugly bullet holes in their pale chests. He touched the stiffened hands and ran his fingers over the half-frozen red places where thumbs had been hacked away.

"Heaven help us," he said lowly.

Rupert grunted disdainfully. "The help we need is a dozen armed men scouring these mountains—or maybe scouring the town would be enough."

Jared turned to him. "What do you mean by that?"

"That maybe we got our killer right here in town. Already caught."

"If you're speaking of Tellico, he was in town when these two were carried in. He couldn't have done it."

"He could have slipped out of town and come back in."

"That's unlikely, as beat-up as he was."

"Were you with him all the time?"

"No."

"Well, then! He could've done it."

Doc interrupted. "Jared, there was a note of some sort?"

Jared nodded. "Pinned to one of the dead men. It was smeared, hard to read." He dug in his pocket and produced a crumpled wad of paper, which he handed to the doctor.

Doc spread it and squinted at the smudged writing on it.

"What's it say?" Rupert asked.

Doc handed the paper back to Jared. "Vengeance," he said.

"Vengeance for what?"

"It doesn't say," Doc responded. He studied the empty spaces where thumbs had been.

No one came to the burial except Isaiah Cable, Jared, Doc, and the stable keeper, Lee Weller. It was interesting, Jared observed, that folks so taken with gawking at the pair when they were laid out in the smithy, now were so indifferent as the snowy earth swallowed the bodies.

Lee was there because it was his job. Along with keeping up the town stable, doing simple carpentry, and cleaning here and there, he customarily dug and filled the graves of Jerusalem Camp. Lee was lanky and long-haired, nearly forty years old, but people still called him boy and always would, for his mental development had stopped in adolescence. With his father dead now for a decade and his mother likewise gone for seven years, Lee lived under the general care of the town as a whole. He survived satisfactorily, residing in a Spartan but snug room built onto the side of the stable. The townsfolk liked him and kept him busy in small-change tasks, though Rupert and Ingersoll made him the butt of pranks when times got dull.

Today, Lee's usual smile was absent, for he was cold. He shivered in the wind, hugging his shovel as if it could warm him. Digging the two graves had generated a sweat that now felt like ice on his forehead.

". . . and receive unto your mercy these two souls, unknown to us but known to you, and this we pray in the name of Jesus Christ, amen."

Jared ran through the prayer rapidly. The snow fell so fast the blanket-wrapped bodies in the holes now wore white shrouds and soon would be hidden altogether if Lee didn't quickly get some dirt on them. Doc muttered an amen and Jared nodded at Lee. The gangly fellow fell to at the dirt pile, his shovel making a steady *chunk-chunk-chunk* as he labored.

Jared scanned the mountains all around them—vast masses of rock and dirt covered with evergreens and smothered in snow. Somewhere out there, he was sure, was the killer of these two men and also of John and Clark Davison. A grim and icy wasteland those mountains were now, not a place one would expect any man to winter. But if he weren't out there, he could only be in the town itself. Jared didn't like to think about that. He thought again of what Rupert had said about Tellico.

Doc pulled his coat more tightly around his thin

body. "I'm heading home before this wind does me in. I feel it in every joint."

"I'll be on shortly myself," Jared said. "I got some thinking to do first."

Doc shuffled down the hill, leaving long furrowed tracks in the snow. Lee, warmed from exertion, was smiling again. He worked with characteristic enthusiasm, moving quickly, eagerly, and with no apparent awareness of the morbidity of his job. His manner reminded Jared of a wiry pup, always eager and cheerfully energetic.

"Never have buried two men at once before, Mr. Jared," Lee said, puffing. "I buried Mizz Jane and her little baby when they died, but I never buried two whole grown-up men at the same time."

"You might be burying more soon," Jared said, mostly to himself. Lee straightened and looked mildly bewildered.

"Is more people going to die, Mr. Jared?"

Jared attempted a reassuring smile. "Maybe not, Lee. Not if I can help it."

"Who killed these men, Mr. Jared?"

Jared shook his head. Then movement at the base of the hill caught his eye. It was Tellico, ascending. The man's lean body moved in an easy flow, only a slight limp giving evidence of his bullet-furrowed leg.

Tellico wore no hat and his hair waved in the cold wind. The steam of his breath immediately scattered into nothingness in the breeze.

"Doc would fuss at you for being out on that leg so quick," Jared said when Tellico reached the graveside.

"I never listen to doctors," Tellico responded, looking at the graves. "Doctor's no good but to put a man in one of these holes while he's still young."

Lee finished his job and grinned heartily at the others, then took his shovel on down the hill.

"Where did you first meet these two, Tellico?" Jared asked.

"In San Francisco. Somehow the story got started that I was carrying money. They followed me for days."

Jared smelled a lie. He faced Tellico more squarely. His eyes flashed like cold glass. "I want to know who you really are, and why you happened to show up in this town just when you did. And why two men who tried to kill you suddenly turn up murdered. Keeping secrets isn't going to help you. It could cause you to end up dead yourself."

"Is that a threat?"

"Of course not. Just a fact. Men like Rupert and Ingersoll aren't as restrained as me. They've got no respect for law, and if they get suspicious enough of you nothing will stop them from doing what they think they have to do."

"In that case, I'll be ready to protect myself," Tellico said.

Then he thrust his hands deep into his coat pockets. He shivered. "I forgot my hat," he said, and strode down the hill toward Jerusalem Camp.

Jared saw him next about one o'clock when he came down from his borrowed shack to Jared's house. Jared watched him through the window as he sat down for his midday meal. Tellico wore his hat now, and his limp was a little more evident. He strode to the door and knocked. Jared rose from the table and answered.

Tellico took off his hat as the door swung open. "Good day, Marshal," he said. "I'd like to talk to you."

Jared waved him in. "Glad to hear it. Come in

and share the meal. Bread and soup is all, but it's hot."

"Obliged."

Anna Cable had not met Tellico until now, though she had heard of him from Jared, and knew he was living in the shack up the hill behind them. She wasn't pleased that Jared had invited Tellico to use their old house, and had told him so, for she was frightened like the rest of the townsfolk and distrusted strangers. She couldn't quite understand why Jared had done it—but then, she never had understood Jared and his impulses.

She greeted Tellico politely if coolly, and Jared introduced his son, Michael, to the newcomer. Michael said hello and stared openly at the visitor.

Tellico looked hungry, but waited with politely restrained impatience as Jared muttered a short prayer. Tellico fell to on the bread like a starved man. He slurped the soup with enthusiasm. Jared and Anna exchanged glances, Jared fighting back a little smile. Michael continued his full-bore stare, to which, Jared noted, Tellico seemed oblivious.

When he was sated, Tellico leaned back in his chair. His eyes swept the three faces before him, and suddenly he was embarrassed. He lowered his gaze to his plate.

"Beg your pardon, ma'am," he said. "It's been quite some time since I sat at a real table, and longer than that since I sat at one with victuals made by such a cook as yourself."

"I'm glad you enjoyed the meal, Mr. Tellico," Anna said. "Did you get enough?"

"I'm satisfied, thank you."

"You will have some pie? Cold, I'm afraid, but sweet."

"Dried apple," added Jared.

Tellico smiled again. "I'd be pleased, Mrs. Cable. I'm not a man to turn down dried apple pie in any circumstance less serious than running for my life."

At that Michael piped in. "Have you done that a lot, Mr. Tellico?"

"Beg pardon?"

"Run for your life. Like from the two who were chasing you with guns."

Jared frowned. "Michael . . ."

"It's all right," Tellico said. "No, Michael. I've not had much experience with that."

"I heard Mr. Rupert knocked you on the head."

"That's enough, Michael," Jared said. "Go eat your pie in the kitchen."

Chagrined, the boy left the room. Jared apologized to Tellico for Michael's inquisitiveness.

"I don't mind it," Tellico said. "Young folk have an advantage over us older ones—no secrets, no deception. Just honest questions and honest statements."

Peculiar talk, coming from a walking secret like yourself, Jared thought. Tellico continued, "I hope you don't mind my coming. I wasn't looking for a meal, but for a job."

Jared frowned. "A job?"

"Yes. I . . ." Anna came into the room, and he cut off. She put slabs of thick, golden-brown pie before the men, and steaming crockery mugs of coffee. The pie swam in cream.

"You're a fortunate man to have such a cook for your bride, Marshal," Tellico said as Anna reentered the kitchen. He said it in just the right way, Jared noticed, while Anna was departing but still within earshot, where she could absorb the compliment without having to put on a responding mask of humility.

"Thank you," Jared said on her behalf. "You were saying . . ."

"Yes. I want to talk to you about a job. If I'm to occupy your dwelling yonder, I owe you something in return. I think I can help you."

"Help me do what?"

"Find the killer stalking this town," Tellico said.

Chapter 4

Jared put down his mug of coffee. "Just how do you propose to help me?"

"Well, how do you plan to find the killer? Whatever your plan, I'll help you carry it out."

Jared smiled ironically. "Maybe I was hoping you would have a plan in mind. Because, frankly, I don't."

"Then let's work together and see if we can come up with one."

Jared took a sip of coffee and thought it over. It was a most remarkable request, made by a man who was, if anything, the closest thing Jared had to a suspect. Was this an attempt by Tellico to cover his own tracks? Maybe, but Jared couldn't really believe Tellico was the killer. It would have required superhuman speed for him to slip away from town, find his two pursuers in the mountains at night, kill them, prop their bodies on their horses, then steer the corpse-bearing horses back into town. Besides, Tellico just didn't strike Jared as a murderous type, and Jared's intuitions about people seldom failed him.

Jared balanced his fears, suspicions, and instincts. "Room and board for you in return—is that what you ask?"

"Yes."

Anna always told Jared he was impulsive. Well, he thought, I'll just live up to that. He nodded. "All right. I'm probably a fool, but let's try it."

Tellico smiled and extended his hand.

Outside, the light grew brighter as the clouds thinned substantially for the first time since the storm had set in. By the time Jared and Tellico had finished their pie and coffee, little strips of blue sky showed through here and there, and the wind diminished.

From the window of the little room where he had sat since early morning, Reverend Isaiah Cable watched the brightening day and gave thanks. His thick, ancient Bible lay across his lap, opened to the Psalms. All morning he had been reading and praying, asking God for a sign of hope, something he could share with the people of his congregation in this time of fear.

"Yea, though I walk through the valley of the shadow," he said to the increasingly blue sky. He smiled, and nodded firmly, shut the Bible, and stood. The old widower still wore the woolen nightshirt he had slept in, and his thin white hair had not been combed all morning. He walked to the mirror and examined his reflection. I'm an old man, he thought. When did I become so old? He looked at himself awhile, then combed back his hair, smoothed his beard, and put on the same dark, heavy woolen clothes he had worn for the past fifteen winters.

Outside, a handful of Jerusalem Camp's men were shoveling pathways through the snow in the street. It was a job they had done for years, and they did it well and quickly, so that when Isaiah was through with his dressing, already a long furrow was cut from his doorway almost to the church. God bless Witt, he always cleared that way first. It was a kindness that Isaiah always appreciated. Seeing Witt up ahead, now almost to the church door as his shovel sent big bites of snow flying, Isaiah hurried, his coattails dusting the edges of the narrow furrow path on both sides.

"Brother Witt, you never fail to bless your old pastor!"

Witt turned, face ruddy with exertion. "Preacher, you spooked me, coming up behind so unexpected!" He grinned. "Then, it might be that I've been a bit jumpy since Jimmy found the dead men."

The preacher shuddered inwardly, his hard-gained good spirits lessening a bit. "Yes," he said. "A hard thing for the boy, no doubt."

"Harder on us grown-ups, I think," Witt said. "Jimmy doesn't understand much what's happening. He thinks it's all rather exciting, I'm afraid."

"Typical boyish feeling."

Witt became very serious. "Preacher, does Jared have any idea who is doing this, or why?"

"I haven't talked to him. But I believe we will see the moving of an almighty hand soon, Brother Witt. God reveals those who do evil."

Witt said nothing, but it was obvious Isaiah's words had given no reassurance. Seeing that, the preacher felt his own confidence slide away to nothing.

"I believe I can wade the snow the rest of the way," he said. "Thank you, my friend, for clearing my path."

"My pleasure, Preacher. When you come out you'll find it clear up to the door."

Isaiah stepped through the snow up to the church, his black coat flapping down, his thin legs rising and falling, making him resemble a crow wading through a deep puddle.

* * *

Lee Weller finished a lunch of cold biscuits with a piece of ham Anna Cable had given him the day before. He wiped crumbs from his mouth onto his sleeve, then went to a wooden box in the corner of his room. Glancing out the window to make sure nobody was looking in, he opened the box and began removing its contents—an old shirt, a torn pair of trousers, pieces of harness, a broken knife—refuse he guarded like treasure.

He lifted out a piece of pine plank that formed a false bottom to the box. From beneath it he pulled a tattered old catalog with pages corn-yellow and brittle. Excitedly he flipped it open, and it fell automatically to the portion he was seeking: several pages of etchings of plump women in various types of underwear. His own secret paper harem.

He sat on his bunk and flipped the pages, back and forth, studying the stiffly posed figures. Then something moved outside his window and he tossed the catalog to the floor, kicked it beneath the bunk, and hid it behind his feet.

Preacher Cable had passed. Walking to the church along the pathway Witt was shoveling. Lee felt a surge of shame; the preacher had not seen what he was doing, but what if he had? Lee had sat through many sermons by Preacher Cable, searing diatribes, eloquent and impassioned condemnations of sin and sinful man that sometimes made Lee wake up in the night feeling hellfire lapping at his feet. If Preacher Cable saw him now, looking lustfully at etchings of women without dresses, it would be almost as bad as if God himself saw him. He wondered if God had eyes like Preacher Cable, the kind that could look warmly at you and make you feel happy and good, or glare at you and open hell beneath your heels.

Lee picked up the catalog, disgusted with himself. I ought to throw it away, he thought, and never think of it again. He balanced the catalog in his hand and options in his mind; then he crept back to his wooden box and sheepishly hid the book away, ashamed he didn't have the moral strength to part with it.

Several minutes later, out in the stable as he cleaned a rear stall, Lee looked up and saw a lone figure at the place where the mountain timber reached the clearing beyond the edge of town. An old man, it appeared, standing so still he might have been carved from wood. He was leaning on a rifle, looking toward the town. Intrigued, the stable keeper watched the figure for a long time, then raised his arm and waved. The old man turned and vanished into the trees.

"So the town was built around the church?" Tellico asked.

"It was," Jared said. "There are four men who are the pillars of Jerusalem Camp, and all of them are churchmen. One is my father, who you'll meet soon—Isaiah Cable, the preacher. Then there's Logan Hull—Doc Hull—one of the church elders. He's the old fellow who examined you. Another is Claude Gregory, another church elder. He ran a dry goods store up until a year ago when he sold it out. He and Matty still live above it. Then there was Jubal Wallen, the last of the four. He's been dead now about a dozen years, and he's buried out behind the church.

"Those four were the founders of this town, and they've kept it going through the years. They put a lot of themselves into it, and when it was first starting they put a lot of their own money in too, until the gold started coming in regularly."

"Your pa must be quite a man," Tellico said.

"He is indeed. I'm mighty fond of him, and proud." Jared paused, thoughtful. "It's hard to see him get old, you know."

"How's he reacting to the murders?"

Jared shook his head. "I haven't talked to him about it. Maybe I'm worried it's more than he can handle. Pa always takes it on himself to be the comforter during hard times. But how do you give comfort for murder?"

Tellico drew a slim cigar from his pocket, walked to the fire, and lit the tobacco with a flaming stick. "This killer—could we track him?"

"Maybe," Jared said. "It depends on the weather and the snow. And on him killing again, which I hope to God he doesn't."

Tellico said, "I'd like to see him caught."

"This not being your town, what's your interest?" Jared asked.

Tellico shrugged. "I'm here for the winter. Guess that makes this my town for now."

"Reckon so. But there's likely to be trouble for you here."

"Rupert and Ingersoll?"

"Right. They'll be suspicious of you until there's proof you're not the killer yourself. Others, too."

"And what do you think, Marshal? You still suspicious of me?"

"No. I suppose not."

"Obliged you trust me."

"Maybe sometimes I trust too many people too much."

Isaiah leaned on the heavily varnished pulpit and looked across the rows of empty pine benches in the church house. The shutters were closed, so sunlight entered the sanctuary in slanting yellow lines between the panels, revealing floating dust and smoke that leaked from the woodstove in the center of the room. Isaiah had built a small fire in it, not enough to really warm the place, but enough to take the edge off the chill. He never built large fires when he came to practice his sermons, which seemed to generate heat on their own.

The sermon he practiced today would be perhaps the most important one since the time, as a much younger preacher in Indiana, he told his congregation of a vision he had: a town high in the mountains to which men would be drawn. The congregation had listened to him then, and responded. Now it was just as important that they listen to him again, and that he give them something worth listening to.

He stood erect and cast his practiced stare over the benches, mentally painting in the familiar faces that would be there come Sunday, each person in his habitual spot. "My brethren," he intoned, "we are passing through the valley of the shadow of death. It is a dark valley, a grim valley. But one well-trodden by the people of God since Abraham left Ur. In that valley, says the psalmist, 'I will fear no evil, for thou . . .' "

The door at the back of the church opened and a man stepped in. About the preacher's age, he was heavy-set, wide-jowled, and very pale. This was Claude Gregory, church elder and close friend of the preacher. Yet he looked so changed and so shaken that for a half-moment Isaiah didn't recognize him. The door shut behind Claude, and in the gloom of the shuttered church house the portly man simply stood there.

"What is it, Claude? You look as if—"

"The thumbs, Isaiah. One thumb cut off each one."

"I know about the thumbs, Claude."

"Then do you see what it means? A cut-off thumb . . ."

Isaiah frowned, thinking, the room silent except for

the hissing of the fire. Suddenly he leaned weakly across the pulpit.

"No," he murmured.

"It has to be, Isaiah. What else could it be? Who else?"

"But he's dead. It's impossible."

Claude sat down heavily on one of the pews. It squeaked beneath him.

"You're right. It is impossible. But the thumbs . . ."

Isaiah spoke with a strained voice. "Let's say nothing of this to anyone."

"Yes. Of course." Claude rose and wearily stepped out the door into the pathway that Witt had shoveled for the preacher.

Chapter 5

Tellico, Jared could tell, was not accustomed to snowshoes. He stomped clumsily along as they traveled the deeply piled hillside toward a little house that stood outside Jerusalem Camp.

"Is this where they died?" Tellico asked as they drew near.

"No. They were hunting out in the mountains. When they didn't come back, Molly—that's John Davison's missus—came into town to get help to find them. Find them they did—a quarter-mile from home, both shot and their thumbs cut off. There was a note with them, but it was wet and the letters had run together so you couldn't read it. Probably said the same thing as the last one."

"So the Davison lady's left alone now."

"Not entirely," Jared said. "She's got one son, Geoffrey, about seven, eight years old. Think what it must be like for him, trying to understand that his pa and his big brother have been slaughtered like pigs."

The house they approached was typical Jerusalem Camp architecture: rectangular, with three windows on the front and one door. Chimneys stood on both ends of the house, marking two fireplaces—one for cooking, one for heating the sleeping quarters on the far end.

They approached the door, Jared deliberately mak-

34

ing a lot of noise so their arrival wouldn't surprise the jumpy widow inside. Since the murders, Molly's unmarried brother, Horace Bailer, had been caring for her. But Horace had a fondness for liquor and spent a lot of time hanging around Rupert's. His horse was gone even now, along with the sledge he used for winter travel. Jared figured Horace right about now was leaning over Rupert's woodstove, warming his hands with the fire and his belly with some cheap whiskey.

Jared rapped on the door, identified himself, and asked for entrance. A moment later the latch moved and rattled and the door creaked open. A woman whose face was forty and eyes were ninety wearily beckoned them in. They doffed their snowshoes and entered.

"Good day, Molly. Horace around?"

"He's in town. Took Geoffrey with him." The woman's voice was a tired slur, devoid of inflection. Jared felt a burst of anger at Horace. He's probably got that boy down there at Rupert's with him while he's getting drunk.

"I'm going to talk to him, tell him you need him here." Jared paused. "Have you heard there were two more killed, same way as John and Clark?"

Horribly, the woman chuckled. "You don't say."

"This time it was two strangers. By the way, Molly, this is Mr. Tellico. He's a new partner of mine, a deputy."

The woman didn't react to the introduction. She plodded to a chair by the window and sat down, resting her elbow on the sill and her chin in her hand, staring out at the snow.

"Molly, we came to check on you and talk to you some about what happened. I know it's not easy, but—"

"I don't care no more. I'll talk if you want."

"Thank you, Molly. Mostly I just want you to think

back over the past weeks, even months. Did John ever have trouble with anybody, make any enemies? Anybody ever threaten him?"

Molly, still staring out the window, shook her head.

"Did he seem nervous or scared anytime before he was killed?"

Same reaction.

"Did he have any hint at all that something was going to happen?"

She suddenly sat straighter, lowered her hand, and looked at Jared. "John didn't have no hint, and neither did Clark. But Geoffrey did."

"Geoffrey?"

"Yes. I only just now remembered it: He knew something was about to happen. For a month he was upset, hardly sleeping, and when he did he had dreams. Bad ones, and they always involved his father."

"Dreams." Jared had hoped for something more substantial to work with than a child's nightmares.

"Yes. His father falling off a cliff—that was one—and his father being mauled by a bear. And other things that weren't so specific, just frightening to a boy. Moving shadows, a face at his window at night, that kind of thing." She mused for a moment. "Funny I should think of it only now. Geoffrey knew. You ever heard of folks just knowing when something's about to happen?"

"I have indeed," Tellico said thoughtfully.

Jared said, "Thank you, Molly. If you think of anything else, let me know. Send Horace down after me."

The woman, momentarily respirited while speaking, now grew old and tired once more. She collapsed into her chair, resuming the same pose as before, watching the winter landscape beyond the window.

When they were going, Tellico paused at the door.

"Mrs. Davison, the face that Geoffrey saw at the window in his dreams . . . what kind of face was it?"

"Didn't say."

They started back over the hill toward town. "Why did you ask that?" Jared said.

"No reason. Just crossed my mind."

Jared said, "Let's knock on some doors. I think it's time for a meeting of the people."

Silent, hidden among the rocks and shadows, the Gray Man watched the town. Watched its rising smoke, the movements of its people, its huddled livestock feeding in pens. He watched boys gathering fuel from woodpiles—working in groups of two or three, rather than singly as before—dogs scampering at their feet. He also saw two men moving from door to door, knocking and speaking briefly to those who answered. They were barely visible in the distance, often hidden altogether. He did not know them or what they were doing, but he guessed it had to do with him and hated them as he hated the entire town.

Heavily dressed in furs, wearing a thick capote over his body and a Balmoral bonnet on his long-unshorn head, he did not feel the cold. His big, oiled boots kept the chill from his feet. He knew mountain life well; survival was no problem. He could move as silently as a cougar and vanish like a ghost.

Through an alleyway between two buildings the Gray Man saw the pair go to another door, knock, and talk to the person who answered. He squinted. This was the same pair, he believed, whom he earlier had watched visiting the house of the first ones he had killed. That house . . . still someone living there.

So far he had taken only four victims; it was time

for another. It really didn't matter who—and that house might provide the best opportunity, for it was relatively remote and hidden from the view of most of the town. Yes. The house would yield him yet another victim.

The Gray Man slipped back into the forest.

Ingersoll pushed open Rupert's sticking door, making it pop and shudder on its hinges. Rupert stood inside, gently rubbing the jaw that Tellico's elbow had pounded earlier; it had been visibly bruised and only now was beginning to look better.

"Loren, you going?" Ingersoll asked.

"Yeah. Yeah, I'm going," Rupert responded. "If the good saints don't mind me dirtying their meetinghouse, that is."

"C'mon, then."

Together the men walked down one of the shoveled-out pathways toward the church down the street. Subsequent snows had partially filled the walkways; keeping them clear would require repeated shoveling until spring. And if the winter brought snows up to thirteen or fourteen feet, as it often did, no amount of shoveling would suffice. Winters like that kept people locked in their homes, free to move about outside only on webbed snowshoes or homemade skis, which the old-timers also called snowshoes.

The street was relatively crowded with people moving single file through the walkways toward the church. Somebody pulled the bell rope, sending rich, purple tones reverberating against the mountains. The lines of people converged at the church door and entered with the solemnity of mourners gathering for a funeral.

Rupert and Ingersoll were among the last in, and finding no seats, leaned against the back wall with a score of others. They looked across the rows of people to Jared, who sat in a chair beside the pulpit, Tellico off in a corner behind him. Tellico looked vaguely nervous and out of place, obviously conscious that he was being scrutinized by the people. Near him was Isaiah Cable, noticeably pale and looking old. Rupert had not seen his old sparring partner for more than a week, and Isaiah's wan, unhealthy countenance was very noticeable to him.

Ingersoll nudged Rupert and subtly pointed at Tellico. "There he is, Loren. Old thumb-chopper himself."

"Yeah. And have you heard—our good marshal's hired him for deputy, to help him solve the killings!"

Ingersoll hadn't heard, but before he could express his surprise Jared stood and walked to the pulpit. He put his hands flat on its sloping top and leaned against it in the universal pose of the uncomfortable public speaker.

"Neighbors, I thank you for coming here," he said. "I'm sorry to put this disturbance in your day, but you know what we're here to talk about."

"When you going to catch him, Jared?" somebody at the front demanded. "There's never been a murder in this town before, and now we've got four of 'em!"

"Well, Claymore, I know that. We all know that. What we don't know is who it is or why he's doing it. It's my opinion that it's somebody outside the town. That's the only way the last two could have been killed. They had never been in town at all."

"Why were they chasing your deputy, Jared?" Claymore Smith asked. "And who is he?"

Every eye turned to Tellico, who looked back across the crowd, unflinching but reading hostility and fear in almost every face.

"This is Mr. Tellico," Jared answered. "He's a man

I trust. The two who chased him were apparently thinking to rob him. It's my opinion they had the bad luck to
run across the killer in the mountains right after that."

Rupert crossed his arms and cocked his left foot
across his right, resting it on its boot toe. "Did you call
us here to tell us your opinions, Marshal, or do you have
some facts for this town?" he said. Then he smiled, enjoying Jared's obvious discomfiture, making Jared hate
him for it.

"If you mean do I have the answers, then no, I
don't," Jared said. "But I do have something to say:
We've got to assume the killings will continue. So
anybody—everybody—is in danger. And our lives are
going to change from now until this is resolved."

"Meaning what?"

"Meaning we're going to start guarding this town
just as carefully as our forefathers guarded their stockades
a century ago," Jared said. "Especially at night. We're
going to organize us a guard militia—not a fool vigilante
gang like you had, Loren—but a group of guards who'll
watch the town in pairs through the night. I want
mounted guards beating a path all the way around town
all night. That's the first thing.

"Second, we're all going to start keeping our eyes
open. Looking out for our neighbors. Checking on the
folks next door. Keeping the women and children in the
company of at least one man all the time. Keeping ourselves sober and our guns loaded. Keeping guns by our
beds. Using our common sense.

"There's a killer loose. We don't know who he is,
where he is, or when he will kill again. It's my fortune,
like it or not, to be the one chosen to provide whatever
protection I can. But I can't do it without the help of
everybody. Can I count on you? Will you work with me
to protect this town?"

Boots scuffed against the plank floor in accompaniment to a murmur of whispers. A woman with a quaking voice said, "Are you saying my children are in danger?"

"Yes, Cora. Yours, mine, everybody's. And you, too."

The woman began to cry; beside her, her young daughter looked up at her. The child's lip began to quiver and then she too was in tears.

"You're upsetting the women and the youn'uns, Jared!" a man said. "Shouldn't this have been talked out in private among the men?"

"The women and children have got to be just as aware of this as the men. And to tell you the truth, I didn't want to leave the women unguarded while we jawed it over."

The crowd thought about that. "You really do believe we're in danger?" the man asked.

"Don't you?" Jared responded.

The man paused, then nodded.

"Thank you. Now what about the rest of you?" Jared raised his right hand and held it high.

All about the room hands rose, until at last even Rupert and Ingersoll joined in.

Suddenly the church doors burst open. The people turned; Horace Bailer stood in the middle of the double doorway. Geoffrey Davison clung to Horace's leg, trembling and crying.

In Horace's arms was Molly Davison. She was bloodied and dead, and her right thumb was missing. Men shouted, women and children screamed, and then the church broke into pandemonium.

Jared closed his eyes and lowered his head for a moment. Then he turned to Tellico and said, "Well, Tellico. It appears you have been exonerated."

Chapter 6

Coal-oil torches flared in the wind but made little impact on the snow-driven darkness. The band of armed men led by Jared winced against the hard flakes that battered their faces and made them numb. Tellico came to Jared and shouted through the blizzard, "It's no use. We lost the tracks. Got to get back."

Jared gave one desperate look around, fought back the frustration that gnarled his stomach, then reluctantly nodded. He turned to the others, who looked like dark ghosts through the bullet-fast snowfall. "Head back!" he shouted, half his volume lost to the wind.

No one argued. The men turned and trudged back toward the town, walking slightly bowlegged in their snowshoes, as if straddling a crack in the ground. Far below, flickering pinpoints of light marked the town. The thought of warmth and firelight drove them on.

Jared mentally cursed the blizzard, which had blasted through only moments after Horace Bailer had appeared with the corpse of Molly Davison. Despite the snow Jared and his quickly formed posse had hurried to Molly's cabin and followed what tracks they could find until the blizzard at last obliterated them.

The returning group entered the west end of the town, stepping over drifts, walking in the rapidly filling remnants of the shoveled pathways. Jared went to his smithy, and several of the others followed.

Inside he built a fire in the forge and blew it hot with the bellows. The men gathered around, extending hands to the blaze, letting heat and orange light play across their frosty faces. They had the look of soldiers the night before battle, or sailors who have seen signs of a hurricane in the eastern sky. There were none who doubted the danger anymore.

"I want to get to my family," Witt Essler said, breaking the silence. "Come get your folks when you're ready, Jared."

Jared, who had left his wife and son with Deb and Jimmy Essler at the Essler house, said, "I'll be on in a few minutes, Witt. Thanks for your help out there."

Others departed too, heading for homes and families, facing a night of lying awake listening for noises in the dark.

At last only Jared and Tellico remained. Despite the roaring fire, Jared was still shivering. Eventually he walked to the window and threw back a sackcloth curtain that once was nearly white but now was charcoal gray with the residue of a thousand smoky fires. He looked at the dark street beyond through the well-frosted windowpane.

"I'm going to get my family and head home," Jared said. "Come stay in our house tonight if you'd feel safer."

"Thank you, but I'll be outside tonight."

Jared realized what, in the excitement of the search, all but Tellico had forgotten. "You're going to guard the town?" Jared asked. Tellico nodded.

"You can't do it alone."

"Sean McFee said he would help me."

"I appreciate you both, then," Jared said. "Most of

the men tonight have enough to think about just watching their own families. Tomorrow night we'll set up guard shifts."

"Glad I can help," Tellico said, and Jared could tell he meant it.

Jared left Tellico at the forge and walked through the darkness toward Witt's house.

Doc Hull heard Jared pass his combined medical office and undertaking parlor. But he kept his attention on the remains of Molly Davison stretched before him on the stained cadaver table. A blanket covered her torso, hiding ugly knife slashes and stab wounds. Doc had examined the corpse carefully; Molly had died a brutal death, killed by someone with powerful arms and a large, very sharp blade. In his time Doc had seen too many corpses to easily become squeamish, but this one bothered him—not because of its gore, but because of who it was and the atrociousness of her murder.

He lifted the blanket and looked again at the wounds. Why? And who? Was the motive somehow related to the Davison family, which now had lost three members to the same killer? But if so, why had the two strangers also been killed? They had nothing to do with the Davisons.

Doc let the blanket fall as he turned away. The right hand of the body flopped out from beneath it and dangled. The place where the thumb had been was raw and red and ugly. Doc reached down and lifted the arm to tuck it beneath the blanket again, but suddenly he stopped.

He stood frozen in place, holding the stiffened wrist while staring at the empty thumb socket. He pushed the hand beneath the blanket, walked away to a corner chair, and sank into it, breathing rapidly, mulling a suspicion too terrible to consider.

Michael and Anna Cable smiled at Jared when he entered the Essler house. Anna appeared close to tears. Michael ran to his father and Jared slipped a burly arm around the boy's shoulders. "Son," he said, "let's go home."

Witt was sipping a cup of coffee. He raised it and said, "Fresh. Want some before you go?"

"I thank you," Jared said. "I am a mite chilled."

Witt disappeared into the kitchen and returned with a mug of coffee that he handed to Jared. At Witt's heel was Jimmy, beaming his gappy grin as if oblivious to the tense adults around him. Deb Essler followed her son, her face like that of a bereaved woman.

Anna smiled tensely at her hostess. "Deb, thank you for your hospitality. I've felt much safer with Michael and me being here with you."

Jared and Witt stood sipping and talking quietly for a few minutes. Finally Jared drained off the last half of his coffee at one swallow. "Thank you, Witt. Deb, you make a good cup. We'll go on now."

Deb took Jared's empty cup, but dropped it. "Damn!" she exclaimed.

Witt, never before having heard his wife curse, gaped at her in amazement. "Deb!"

Her chin quivered, then tears came. She turned on Witt like a lioness.

"What? You never heard your wife talk like that before? Well, listen again: Damn! Damn it all! There! I've said it and it feels good. I'm sick of living with this tension and not letting it out! Damn!"

Jimmy's eyes were big in his face like twin full

moons. He grinned. "Thay it again, Ma!" he urged. "Thay the bad word!"

Witt grew angry. "Deb, you're not fit to be in the presence of decent company. What's gotten into you?"

"Let's go," Jared uncomfortably mumbled to his family. Then to Witt, "It's a tense time for everybody. We take no offense that—"

"Oh, you take no offense?" Deb said mockingly. "Your preacher's-son ears don't take offense to a fool woman's babbling? Then hear some more from her: When are you going to do something about these killings, Marshal?" The last word dripped sarcasm. "Who's next to die? Me? My son? My husband? What are you going to do?"

Jared's face went red. "I'm doing what I can, Deb."

"And a lot of good it did Molly! You left her alone in that cabin to be slaughtered like a cow! Who's next?"

Jared swallowed, with much effort holding in a sudden surge of anger. Witt stepped between Deb and Jared.

"Get to the bedroom, Deb. Now!"

Crying, she turned and stalked back through the house. A door slammed, and the sound of muffled sobs followed.

"I'm sorry, Jared," Witt said.

"It's all right, Witt." He swallowed. "Maybe she's right. I didn't do Molly any good. I did leave her alone."

Witt shook his head. "You left her alone, Tellico left her alone, her brother left her alone, she left herself alone. Nobody—you, me, her family—protected her. If you want to toss out blame, then toss it out to everyone. Just don't take it all yourself."

"Thanks, Witt. I wish that made me feel better."

"None of us is going to feel better until this killer is caught, Jared."

"Yeah. Good night, Witt."

The open door cast a beacon of yellow across the snow. The storm had diminished to flurries. The Cables stepped into it and the door closed behind them, cutting off both the light and what Jimmy was saying to his father: "Ma thaid the D word, Pa. Just like Mither Rupert . . ."

Any other time Jared would have laughed. Not tonight.

In silence the family returned to their house. Jared built up the fire, put Michael to bed, and checked the bars on the doors and shutters. He brewed coffee in the pot that hung on a hinged arm in the fireplace. Anna went into their room and came out in the blue calico gown Jared had given her for Christmas a year before. She had a heavy shawl over her shoulders, and Jared could see she had been crying in secret.

Jared swallowed some of the coffee, swirled the remainder in the bottom of his cup, then suddenly tossed it into the fire. The hiss made Anna jump.

"Why, Anna? Why am I the one everybody expects to catch this—this whoever-he-is, wherever-he-is killer? I'm a blacksmith, blast it! I'll not take the blame for not being a proper marshal when I never asked for the lousy job in the first place! Pretty soon everybody in town will be blaming me, just like Deb did."

He waited for Anna to speak, but she didn't. Her silence was grim. He wheeled toward her.

"You blame me too?"

She looked surprised and hurt. "Of course not! I just don't know what you want me to tell you."

Jared leaned against the mantelpiece, forcing himself to calm down. "I want you to tell me that if I go to bed and sleep long enough, it all will go away and everything will be all right again."

"Maybe it will."

Jared shook his head. "No. I wish it would. But it won't."

He paced about the room. Anna returned to the bedroom. A few minutes later Jared lifted his head with a start. "Pa!" he said. "I got to see to Pa!"

He couldn't believe he hadn't thought of it before. Isaiah, down there alone, and him up here feeling sorry for himself. Not only a poor marshal, but an even worse son.

He had just started back to get Anna and Michael when a knock on the front door startled him. He went to the fireplace, slid his shotgun off the mantel hooks, then carefully opened the door.

It was Tellico. Dusted with snow, he carried the rifle Jared had loaned him. Beside him stood Isaiah, huddled in his coat, two blankets and a bag in his arms.

Tellico said, "I thought you'd want him with you tonight. You'd have thought of it yourself if you didn't have so much on your shoulders." He touched his hat. "I'll see you in the morning."

He trudged off, his snowshoes shuffling as he vanished in the night. He didn't seem so clumsy on them now.

Jared and his father talked for a time, but Isaiah seemed reluctant to say much, and soon went to bed in the spare room. Jared went to the window and opened the shutter. He sought Tellico's form there in the darkness, and finally made it out. Tellico stood on a rise a hundred yards away, where he had a good view of the town. A sudden break in the attenuated clouds let moonlight stream through. Tellico, with his rifle cradled in the crook of his arm, suddenly seemed otherwordly and magnificent as he watched over the cluster of snowy rooftops and smoking chimneys below.

Jared was very tired. He closed the shutters and

went to bed. He curled up close to Anna and listened to the snores of his father in the next room. He closed his eyes.

He didn't feel as edgy as before.

Tellico was out there. Tonight, at least, the town would be safe.

Chapter 7

The morning broke clear and pure. Jared, up early, watched the eastern sky grow pale and luminescent until suddenly the sun burst over the rocky summits and poured light into the enclosed valley of Jerusalem Camp. The morning lessened the hopelessness of the night before. Jared dressed, pulled on his boots, and ate a good breakfast, ready to begin the day.

He trudged up the hill on his snowshoes toward Tellico's shack. The sight of Tellico on the knoll during the night, rifle on his arm, had removed any remaining doubts about Tellico's character. Jared congratulated himself on his good instincts. He had sensed almost from the beginning that Tellico was a man he could trust, despite his aggravating secrecy about himself.

He reached Tellico's door and lifted his fist to knock. He noticed, though, that the door was not fully shut. He grew cautious. Quietly he pushed open the door.

"Tellico?" he said softly.

He heard soft snores from the bedroom and approached. It was Tellico, sleeping soundly. He apparently had merely failed to shut the door completely when he came in. Probably he had been exhausted from his sentry duty.

Jared turned to leave, not wanting to disturb a man who had so earned a good rest. But he noticed again the medallion that hung around Tellico's neck. He wondered why Tellico wore such an unusual ornament, and what it meant.

As Jared went back down the hill, he saw his father ahead of him, walking toward the church. Jared hurried, and by the time Isaiah was struggling to open the door against snow drifted upon it, Jared had caught up with him.

"Let me get that, Pa," he said, pulling open the door. "Dadgum snow can be heavy. You ought to be careful to—" He looked at his father's face and stopped, stunned. "Pa, are you all right?"

Isaiah looked at his son with an expression so grim and hopeless that it belied his words: "I'm fine. I've just got a sermon to prepare."

He entered and closed the door. Jared stood overwhelmed by the thought Isaiah's changed face had roused: My father is dying.

Jared saw Rupert on the porch of his store. Rupert waved him over. Bracing for the worst as he always did when dealing with Rupert, Jared trudged over.

"Come inside, Jared. It's plenty warm in here." Jared was surprised by the unusual friendliness of Rupert's tone, and that he had called him by name rather than his usual sarcastic "marshal" or "blacksmith."

Rupert gave Jared a chair by the stove and a cup of coffee. Then Rupert sat down across from him, leaned forward in his chair, and began talking intently, almost whispering.

"Jared, you and me and your pa have had our differences. I'll never be a psalm-singer, and your pa won't ever warm to an old sin-seller like me. You neither, I'd guess. But the fact is, Jared, I've always liked you. No, don't give me that look—it's true. I've just always been expected by folks to fuss at you and your pa, and so I have.

"But now I want to help you. When I saw Horace at that church door with Molly in his arms it made me see what this town is up against. All of us. I want to bury the hatchet with you and help you find whoever is doing this."

Jared, amazed at what he was hearing, nodded. "Thank you, Loren. I need your help. I need every available man to take a shift at guard duty at night."

Rupert shook his head. "That's not what I mean. I want to go for help. Get the law, the real law. Don't take offense at that, but you know what I mean."

Jared nodded. "Yes, I do. But how can you get through the pass? You'll just get buried under an avalanche."

Rupert licked his lips. He drifted back in memory. "When I was a younger man I was mighty good on snowshoes. I won my share of races, you know."

Skis—or snowshoes, as some still called them—had opened the High Sierras to settlement. In the first days of the mountain towns, winter snowfall had driven the miners back down to the foothills to wait out the snow, but Scandinavians soon taught them the art of skiing. From then on the mountains remained populated even through the worst winters, when snow would pile to the rooftops and drifts would reach thirty or more feet.

Jared had heard that Rupert, in younger days, had been an excellent skier. But that was thirty years ago. What Rupert obviously was offering was infeasible at best, crazy at worst. But Jared was touched by Rupert's desire to help.

"Loren, I appreciate that offer more than you can know. But I can't accept it. Too dangerous. Besides, what can anybody from the outside do that we can't? We can search the valley better than anybody, and guard ourselves better than outside law."

Jared said it as diplomatically as he could, but Rupert was offended. He seemed to withdraw into himself.

"Maybe you're right," he said. "Just a fool idea from an old man."

"Don't put words in my mouth, Loren. I really do appreciate your offer."

After Jared left, Rupert sat by his stove, lost in thought. Finally he got up and went to a rear storage room and found two long, homemade skis and a thick wooden balance pole. He ran his hands over the smooth wood, then nodded resolutely.

"Got some preparing to do," he said aloud.

For the rest of the day he was busy, and when the next morning came, he was gone.

As Jerusalem Camp slept that night, two guards circled the town in opposite directions as Tellico rode the maze of snow-and-mud gulleys that comprised the streets. He was under no duty to ride guard tonight, but he had nothing better to do, and he couldn't sleep.

Typical of mountain mining communities, Jerusalem Camp had been built with no apparent design, so that what at one place looked like a good-running street would suddenly be blocked off by a building and the street would veer like a stream around a boulder. The main street was the only straight one in town, and the only reason for that was Isaiah's insistence. "It isn't fitting for the house of God to stand on a crooked way," he had said. "He makes the crooked ways straight, and this one shall be."

Tellico was pleased with the horse and rifle Jared had loaned him. Tellico had a good feeling about Jared. He was solid, unassuming, levelheaded. The kind of man who could weather a tough crisis despite his own feeling that he couldn't. That was part of his very strength. Tellico had known many men over the years who thought themselves weak when in fact they were strong, and others who thought themselves strong when really they were weak.

He had known both types in life and in death. Through his mind flashed memories he despised: bloody, mangled soldiers in tattered blue uniforms, crying in pain, not wanting to live but afraid to die. He remembered holding the clammy hands of such men, saying words into their faces that they didn't hear. He recalled the frustration that had brought, and what frustration had finally led him to do.

He halted his mount and looked around the town. "Jerusalem Camp, what am I doing here?" he asked aloud. Well, why not here? If not here, then somewhere else just as meaningless.

But maybe not. Nothing happens without design, he once had believed, maybe still did. If so, he wondered what design it was that had brought him to Jerusalem Camp, and what its result would be.

He spurred his mount and began slowly winding through the snowy streets again.

Chapter 8

Sunday morning, and Jared stood outside the church, dreading to enter. The body of Molly Davison lay inside in an open pine box, her pale hands carefully placed to cover the missing thumb. There would be no traditional Sunday morning sermon today; this would be a funeral service.

Jared looked up on the hillside; Lee Weller labored there, just now finishing his grave-digging. Unusual thing, for Lee seldom fell behind in his work. But even the simpleminded Lee had been sad and preoccupied since Molly's murder.

Anna came to the door. "It's about to start, Jared."

"All right."

Jared found a seat in the back. Though the church was filled with its usual attendants, there was no feeling of communion here tonight. The very air was oppressive. It was more like a gathering of prisoners than anything else.

He saw his father's face, and his heart dropped to the pit of his stomach. The aging preacher seemed a caricature, or an animated wax figure.

Isaiah stood behind the pulpit and looked over his congregation. He spoke in a voice lacking its normal booming, sonorous timbre.

"Beloved people," he said. "We come to lay to rest

the body of one we have loved. And to ask a question
with no answer: Why?"

Jared heard a sniffle, then a muffled sob. It's starting
already, he thought. I don't think I can stand a lot of
crying and nose-blowing—especially with Pa looking
half-dead like that.

". . . Evil has come upon us, unexplained, and taken
the life of an innocent lady. Who can understand the
strength of evil? Who can know either the ways of God
or the ways of the wicked one? Who can . . ."

Jared rose and slipped out the door. Let the funeral
go on without him. He had enough to put up with. Once
outside, he breathed deeply and enjoyed the cold air
against his face. Inside the church the stove belched
near-hellish heat, the kind to dry a man's throat and turn
his eyes to sand. The cold felt better.

Jared smelled tobacco smoke and heard a cough. In
the alley between the church and the Smith & Wilson
leather goods store stood Lee, puffing a big cigar, hacking
and coughing.

"I didn't know you smoked, Lee."

"I don't. Not most the time. But they say it makes
you feel better."

"If you're used to it. If you're not you just get sick."

"I want to feel better. I'm scared."

"Everybody's scared, Lee."

"The man's going to come kill me. I know he is."
Lee seemed on the brink of tears.

"You don't know that."

"I do too know it. I'm bad and he's going to kill
me."

Jared asked, "What do you mean, bad? You're a
good man."

"But . . ." Lee looked down. The cigar trembled in
his fingers. "I got bad pictures I look at sometimes."

Jared had to think that over to make sense of it. He smiled. "Lee, God bless your heart, you're probably the most guiltless man in Jerusalem Camp."

The words went right past the simpleminded man, who now leaned against the side of the church as the tobacco got to him. "But I'm bad, and he's going to kill me."

Suddenly the church door flew open; Witt thrust out his head.

"Jared, your father's collapsed."

Jared rushed inside. In the alley, Lee lost his fight with the cigar and emptied his stomach with great cramping heaves.

Doc Hull put his arm on Jared's shoulder.

"He's alive, but it's affected him. You'll see he won't talk as plainly, and that his right side is a little paralyzed. You'll notice it most in how his mouth droops. But there's no reason I can see he shouldn't recover quickly."

"What caused it, Doc?"

"Who can say? Age, health, anxiety. Just be grateful he's alive. It could have killed him."

On the bed Isaiah looked even more corpselike than before. His white hair bushed out from the back of his head around his ears. The right side of his mouth drooped.

"Pa, it's Jared."

The old man's heavy-lidded eyes shifted sideways. He looked at his son with a strange and wild glare.

"You're going to be all right. You're in my house, and we're going to take care of you."

The preacher did not try to talk. Jared reached across and patted his hand, but Isaiah didn't seem to notice.

After a few minutes he was asleep. Jared slipped out of the room. Anna waited in the kitchen.

"You need to resign as marshal," she said. "You can't deal with protecting this town and with taking care of your father, too."

"I can't resign, Anna. Not now."

"It never should have been your problem to begin with. You only took the job because they asked you!"

"But that's the point. I took it."

Surprisingly to Jared, Anna grew angry. She spun on her heel and went back to their bedroom. The door slammed.

Jared shook his head and lifted his eyes. "Oh, God, help me now," he said. "If ever I needed it, it's now."

A few minutes later, Tellico appeared at his door. "Can you talk for a minute?"

Jared nodded and left the house. He and Tellico walked through the snow together. Tellico expressed his regrets about Isaiah, then dropped news that hit Jared like a boulder.

"Loren Rupert's gone," he said.

"What?"

"Gone. Not a trace of him. His store's locked, everything in its place. But he's gone."

Jared felt a surge of dread. "Another victim."

"I don't think so. Ingersoll said Rupert had been talking about trying to ski out for help."

"That's right . . . he said the same to me, in fact. But I never thought he'd really do it."

"He seems the kind to do what he wants," Tellico said.

"He does, at that. The old fool! He'll get himself killed."

"How can he get out? I thought the pass was impossible to get through."

"It is, without a whole heap of luck," Jared said.

Across the snowbound town, plumes of gray smoke rose from chimneys and wafted into the clouds. The two men watched.

Tellico seemed to be thinking. At last he said, "Do you believe in fate, Marshal? Or providence or destiny or whatever you want to call it?"

"I suppose I do. Why do you ask?"

Tellico smiled and shrugged. "I don't know. Just thinking out loud."

Rupert wasn't sure, but he thought he had cracked a rib. It sure as the devil felt like it. He had rolled a long way over a drop he hadn't even noticed until it was too late to stop.

He gripped his side and grimaced in pain, struggling to breathe. Jared had been right; he was too old to have tried this. Too late now. He was at least three miles from Jerusalem Camp, one of his skis was gone, and he was hurting so badly he doubted he could make it on foot back to the town. He had his web snowshoes strapped to his back, but they would do him no good if he couldn't bear to stand.

But he couldn't lie here, either, and freeze to death in the snow. It wouldn't be long until dark and he had been here for an hour. He had to find shelter.

Straining, he reached around and pulled his pack from beneath him. He tugged it open and removed a spare shirt. He pushed upward, unsuccessfully tried to squelch a yell of pain, then sat panting, hurting with every heave of his lungs.

Got to go on. Can't stop.

With herculean effort, Rupert slid off his heavy coat. He wrapped the extra shirt around his middle and pulled it tight, binding up his damaged rib cage. Then, with great discomfort, he put on the coat again and donned the snowshoes.

He still had his balance pole, thank God. Dreading what faced him, he closed his eyes and tried to will away as much pain as possible. Finally, with teeth gritted, he began pulling himself to his feet, using the balance pole as a crutch.

At last he was firmly planted upright. His right knee throbbed with pain, and his ribs ached. Wincing, he began walking.

He looked about for any kind of shelter—a cave, a closely bunched stand of pine, an overhanging outcrop. But he found nothing.

It was becoming colder. His ribs and knee hurt worse than before.

I'm still alive, he reminded himself. Got to hang on. Keep moving.

Time dwindled away. His mind drifted into limbo, and his feet moved along as if of their own accord. He lost all concept of distance.

Thus he had no idea how far or long he had traveled when he saw the cabin. He topped a modest slope, and there it sat below him, nestled by a little stream, belching smoke from its stick chimney.

Rupert was so grateful he cried.

He moved on down the slope. He made it to the door and everything began to grow unreal. His pain suddenly vanished; he became warm, content. . . .

When he awoke, a face looked back at him. A man about thirty-five, with hard eyes and bright red hair that hung to his shoulders. Rupert was in a stupor. The thought crossed his mind that he might be dead, and this might be his personal angel. Or devil.

"Hello," he said, scratchy voiced. "My name's Rupert."

The red-haired man leaned close. "Ye got any money, old man?"

Chapter 9

Doc Hull slowly climbed the stairs to Claude and Matty Gregory's apartment above the dry goods store. At the top he paused for a minute to pant, and ponder the cruel things age does to a man. Then he knocked.

Matty answered. Usually jovial, today she was somber. The meager smile that did flit across her lips was pure formality and it showed. But she stood back and invited Doc inside politely enough.

The interior of the apartment smelled mustily of baked bread, closed windows, and moisture. A drab, sunfaded elegance permeated the place, perpetuated by Matty's constant dusting and sweeping. Neat but aging cloths circled with decorative hanging knots covered every table and stand, and pictures were everywhere: Jesus feeding the multitudes, Washington at Valley Forge, plump women in translucent clothing doing a pagan dance around a pole while mythological gods looked down from the clouds.

"Where's Claude?" Doc asked.

"Lying down." Matty's voice was weaker than usual. "He's done poorly these past days."

"I'll take a look at him."

"Well, Doc, to tell you the truth, Claude really doesn't want to see anybody."

"I think I know why. I've got to see him, Matty. There's no choice."

Claude didn't really seem ill, just depressed. He turned his face away from Doc and toward the papered wall. Doc stood beside Claude's bed until finally Claude had to look at him.

"I'd like to talk to him in private, Matty," Doc said.

"Well . . ."

"It's all right," Claude muttered. "Go on."

Matty reluctantly left the room. The door clicked behind her.

Doc smiled sadly at Claude. "Claude, we've got a problem."

"I don't know what you're talking about."

"I think you do. The chopped thumbs, Claude. What do they remind you of?"

Claude twisted his lip downward in a bitter scowl. He aimed it at Doc in silence.

"Isaiah collapsed, you know," Doc said. "I think he had figured it out too."

Claude said nothing of his encounter with Isaiah in the church.

"We can't pretend this is going to go away by itself, Claude."

Claude said, "If you're saying what I think you are, you're insane. That whole sorry event is thirty-five years dead and buried."

"Then why are you hiding away up here in your bedroom?"

Claude glared at Doc. "I'm feeling poorly. I'm an old man."

"We're all getting old, Claude."

Claude asked his next question hesitantly. "Are you going to say something about this to anyone?"

Doc thought it over. "It would be the honorable thing to do. If these deaths are even indirectly our fault . . ." He stopped for a moment. "But no. Not yet. Not until I'm sure."

"It can't be him, Doc. We saw him dead."

"We saw him shot and buried. Maybe not dead."

Claude rolled over to face the wall again. Doc went out and spoke his good-bye to Matty.

"Don't come around upsetting him anymore," Matty said. "I don't like it."

"Neither do I," Doc replied. He left the apartment and walked stiffly down the stairs to the alley.

The face of the man with the red hair was masked in anger. Rupert's ears rang from the repeated backhand blows the man had laid on his jaws.

"Where did ye see Tellico?" the man demanded again.

Rupert had let the information slip bit by bit, against his own will through the persuasion of torture. Rupert had no devotion to Tellico and did not consider it his duty to protect him from this man who obviously wanted him so badly—but Rupert despised the notion of being forced to do anything.

"Go to the devil," Rupert muttered.

The red-haired man snarled; his brawny hand went up and down again, and Rupert had to struggle to retain consciousness.

Then the man stopped. He scrutinized his prisoner.

"All right, then," he said. "Old Frank Coop's a gentle man by nature, but ye ain't cooperating."

He pressed on Rupert's broken ribs. Rupert screamed and passed out.

When he struggled back to awareness, Coop's face

was mere inches above his. "Where did ye see Tellico?" he asked once more.

Rupert could hold out no longer.

"In Jerusalem Camp. Jerusalem Camp."

The brows lowered. "Where's that?"

"Yonder way . . . three, four miles northwest." Rupert's voice was strained. He hurt so badly that the thought of being killed wasn't nearly as troubling as before.

"Four miles northwest," the man repeated. He stood straight and grinned.

"Help me," Rupert whispered.

But the man did not notice him. He began gathering supplies. When he was through, he put on his hat, extinguished the fire, and went to the door. He put on Rupert's webbed snowshoes.

He opened the door, turned, and drew his pistol. He aimed it at Rupert's head, squinting one eye. Then he lowered the weapon.

"No point in wasting a bullet when the cold will do the job just as good."

He thumbed down the hammer, holstered the rusty weapon, and walked out, leaving open the door. Through it blew cold air that stirred the ashes in the fireplace into a cloud of gray dust.

Tellico scanned the mountains as he walked up the slope toward the vacant cabin of Molly Davison. Horace Bailer had moved out after his sister's murder, turned the care of little Geoffrey over to another family, and taken refuge in liquor. He hardly showed himself about town, hiding away instead in a little rented room for which everyone knew he could not and would not pay. There Horace drank, starting early and ending late.

Tellico shifted his rifle and concentrated on his walking. If his time in Jerusalem Camp had taught him anything so far, it was that life in snowy mountains took a lot of endurance. A few strides in the snow and a man was nearly winded. That thought brought another: What kind of man must the killer be, living out in those wild mountains as he was? He must have had years of experience in the wilderness.

Tellico reached the Davison cabin and stopped to get his breath. He had come here on an impulse. Something Molly had said about Geoffrey's dreams of a face at his window had set him thinking.

He tried the cabin door, knowing it would be locked. But it wasn't.

The latch moved in his hand and the door swung open. Cautiously, Tellico looked inside. Dusty rays slanted through the shadowed room. His eyes were drawn to the floor, where a brown crust showed the spot where Molly had died. He wrinkled his nose and averted his eyes.

Not a sound came from within the cabin. The place was ransacked, but Tellico did not know if it had happened at the time of the murder or later. Frowning, he quietly stepped inside.

For a long time he stood there listening and looking. Then he walked through the cabin, the floor creaking, his breathing tense and tight. At every corner he stopped, then moved around it quickly with his rifle ready. But he found no one there.

Within moments he had checked all the rooms but a small one in the back. The door was shut.

He approached it slowly, his rifle leveled at his hip, cocked and ready. A yard from it he froze; he heard a tapping noise, very faint, from the other side of the door.

Tellico's heart raced. His throat went tight and sand-dry. Steeling himself, he coiled his muscles, then drove forward, kicking open the door.

It burst back into an empty room. Tellico leapt inside, turning this way and that, almost firing when he saw a form before him and failed to realize for a moment that it was his own reflection in a full-length mirror. This was a bedroom. He looked in the wardrobe and beneath the bed. Nobody was here.

He stood, relieved. Then it hit him.

Tobacco smoke. The smell hung in the air. Somebody had been here only a few minutes before.

He went to the window, which was not quite shut. The unlatched shutters accounted for the tapping noise he had heard. Tellico raised the window, pushed open the shutters, and saw tracks in the snow.

Somebody on snowshoes. A light snow was falling, and the tracks were slowly filling, but they remained clear for the moment. He stared at them, suddenly wishing they were not there. He thought about turning away, pretending he had not seen them, and returning to town. Let Jared handle this job. After all, he was the appointed marshal, and Tellico was just a newcomer, here almost by chance. . . .

No.

He had asked for this task, and he would see it through.

Tellico left through the front door and circled the house to where the tracks angled up the slope, cutting through the tamarack. Whoever had made the tracks had been careful to keep hidden behind the house. The tracks weren't too far apart; the man was not especially tall, nor was he heavy.

Tellico proceeded cautiously, though the amount of

new snow in the tracks indicated his quarry was far ahead. Still, the farther Tellico got from town, the more vulnerable he felt.

The rise became more extreme and rocky. The path narrowed. Eventually Tellico had to wind up a narrow gully extending up the mountain.

The sky grew more cloudy. Both the higher elevation and the rising wind made him cold, though the heat of exertion compensated somewhat for it. At last the pathway widened again and he came out into an area of barren rock.

Here the wind was incredibly strong. Over the years it had gnarled the trees so they looked like arthritic hands groping out from the mountainside. There were no tracks here.

Sweating, tired, with no sign to follow, Tellico paused on the windy rock face to gather his strength. Some minutes later he turned and began his trek downward.

Behind him moved a flash of gray and white. He whirled. Nothing. Perhaps it had been only a bird flitting over a gray boulder, or the wind-shaken branches of one of the stark trees.

Near the bottom of the mountain he stopped. Something lay in the snow. He hadn't noticed it on the way up, but it must have been there, judging from the amount of snow covering it.

It looked like a small book. He picked it up and dusted the snow from it. It was leather-bound, and inside was a portrait of a woman.

A chill shivered down his spine. This could have belonged only to the one he had tracked up the mountain.

Tellico tucked it into his pocket. Jared would want to see this. Occasionally he removed it and looked at it as he continued. Something about it teased at his mind, but he couldn't quite figure it out.

By now the sun was swollen at the rim of the western mountains, sliding down the sky. Tellico hurried, passing the Davison cabin and its window where little Geoffrey had seen a face that Tellico now was sure had been no dream at all.

His snowshoes kicking a white cloud, he entered the town and walked along its main street, grateful to be among buildings and people again.

Chapter 10

Louis Brooks was a strapping man nearing thirty, known throughout the camp as a fine marksman, a lucky placer miner, and a deacon of the Jerusalem Camp church who was sincere if not sophisticated. Tonight he rode counterclockwise around the random cluster of buildings that comprised the town, and pondered what a drab place it was. For him that was a novel revelation. Louis seldom ventured beyond his house after dark and usually saw Jerusalem Camp only by the more flattering light of day.

The butt of his well-oiled Spencer rifle rested against his thigh, the barrel pointed skyward. His circling, and the simultaneous clockwise circling of Sean McFee, had beaten into the snow a clear path that his horse followed without guidance.

Louis shifted his weight and smiled. He couldn't dare let anyone know it, but he was enjoying this. There was something exhilarating in riding guard; it fulfilled secret longings that Louis had coddled since childhood. He had missed military service, never encountered a hostile Indian, never seen an authentic outlaw or gunman, and because of his size and the peaceable nature of the people among whom he had been raised, had never even been called out to fight. It was very frustrating.

Louis had always longed to be heroic, but until now he had never had a chance.

Sean rounded the rear corner of the little book and confections store on the southwestern corner of town. His white stallion was almost invisible against the snow, making Sean appear to float like a ghost.

"Anything?" Sean asked as he passed.

"Nope."

"Good thing."

It was the same thing he had said every round, fifteen of them so far. Sean made something predictable out of everything he did.

After a while, Louis softly began whistling a nameless old folk tune and slumped in his saddle. This was too blamed easy. He knew that Jared and his newcomer deputy were convinced the town was in perpetual danger, but he was beginning to doubt it. The notion of a killer hidden in the mountains struck him as unlikely. He had his own suspicion: Horace Bailer. The old drunk probably had some personal grudge that he took out on his kin. As for the two murdered strangers, they probably were just a diversion from the obvious.

Here came Sean again. Louis rode past him. A few yards beyond, he halted his mount and turned.

Sean hadn't said his expected line.

"Sean?"

The white horse plodded on. Sean didn't turn.

Louis wheeled and went after him. He pulled up beside him. Sean stared straight ahead. He didn't blink.

"Sean, are you . . ." Louis's words choked off, for when he touched Sean's arm, the silent man slid slowly off his saddle into the snow. Sean's right thumb was gone.

Cold as he was, a sweat erupted on Louis's forehead. He backed away and opened his mouth to yell.

Something sharp touched his neck—just a slight sting, like a needle probe. But it took his voice. He reached to his throat and stared in disbelief at his hand when he pulled it away again, for it was drenched in brilliant blood.

Somebody had cut his throat.

He turned as weakness overcame him, and the last thing he saw was the gray figure and long knife that lanced forward like a sting. He fell from the saddle into the snow; the Gray Man loomed above and the knife came down again, again.

The Gray Man severed Louis's thumb and moved into the town, creeping silently into the alleyway between the millinery and the bank.

Horace Bailer turned the bottle upside down and shook its last drop onto his tongue. He licked the back of his teeth, wiped his mouth on his sleeve, and smashed the bottle against the iron stove. Fragments landed in a heap.

Horace paced around the room in a tight circle, shaking, wringing his hands before him and then clasping them behind. This was his routine since Molly's death —drinking and pacing.

Molly's death. His fault. He should never have left her alone.

He needed another bottle. But how to get one? All businesses were closed, Rupert was missing and his place locked tight, and besides, it wasn't safe for a man to go out on the streets with people so fearful.

But I got to have a bottle. Got to.

He went to the window and pulled back the curtain. He saw Red Pringle out there with his shotgun.

Small, wispy clouds scudded across the sky like roaches on a pantry floor. They blocked the moon for one moment, let it shine through the next. Horace looked across the street just as the latest passing cloud unveiled the moon again and illuminated the false front of the Jerusalem Camp Gun Shop. That reminded him: Curly kept several bottles of good whiskey hidden away under a cabinet in there, slipping drinks from them when Isaiah and other church folk had their backs turned. And that back door of Curly's hadn't had a working lock in four years.

Got to have a drink. Curly won't care.

Red was gone now, somewhere on the other end of town. Horace was nervous about going out onto the street. But he could almost smell Curly's good whiskey. He went to the pile of dirty clothes in the corner and pulled out his coat, hat, and old boots.

The snow crunched beneath his feet, sucked at his boot soles with each step. He dug his hands into his pockets and trudged out into the main street, watching for Red. He hurried on as fast as snow and drunkenness would let him.

Sure enough, Curly still hadn't fixed the lock. The door swung open and Horace entered. He clicked the door shut and squinted into the darkness. Long rifles shone dimly in what little moonlight came in through the windows, pointing toward the ceiling in their neat oak racks along the walls. Powder casks and small kegs of solvent and gunstock finish sat at his feet. The shop smelled of oiled metal. Through the grate on Curly's stove Horace saw the remnants of the day's fire, a faint throbbing red beneath a blanket of ash.

He extended his hands to it, burning off the chill. Cozy place Curly kept here, still warm despite being closed for hours. Maybe Curly wouldn't mind if he curled up later in a corner and slept off the whiskey he would drink.

Whiskey. In which cabinet was it? He rummaged around, groping among dismantled firearms and strangely shaped gunsmithing tools until his hand touched cold glass. Smiling, he pulled out a half-full bottle of good rye. God bless you, Curly.

Fifteen minutes later Horace was in a near-stupor, wonderfully warm and content. He hugged the bottle like a lover, breathing slowly and deeply as he sat against the wall beneath the rear window. He raised the bottle and wrapped his lips around its mouth. As more liquor drained into his throat, something passed the window above him and cast a shadow across the floor beyond his feet.

Horace froze. The distorted shadow on the floor revealed a man was looking in the window. Horace watched with childlike fear, feeling like the shadow itself could see him. But the little part of his mind that remained lucid told him he was surely not seen, that his location directly below the window hid him. So he sat still, clutching his bottle, and tried not to breathe too loudly.

The shadow remained.

Frightening realizations came; he glanced about at the other windows, at the door that would not lock, and knew that if he couldn't be seen from the window above him, he certainly could be seen from the others if the silent watcher moved. Oh Lord, I'm a sinful man. I'll throw away the liquor if you'll keep me safe. Throw it away forever, Lord, or at least for a day.

The shadow vanished. For a moment Horace was relieved. Then he saw it again, this time outside the door.

He slid frantically across the floor, horribly scared, looking for cover. The latch clicked and the door moved slowly, gliding open on hinges lubricated with gun oil.

Horace pulled himself under a table as the open doorway silhouetted a man's form. The man reached down to loosen his snowshoes, then stepped in, heels clumping on the hardwood floor.

Horace tried not to whimper. From beneath the table he watched the feet step across the floor and stop where the bottle of rye lay dropped, just now spilling the last of its contents onto the floorboards.

A hand descended and picked up the bottle. Then a voice: "Horace, you in here somewhere?"

Red. Thank God in heaven. Just old Red Pringle.

"I'm here, Red. I'm real sorry I busted in. I really am. I just needed a drink."

Red stooped and looked beneath the table. "Horace, I could've shot you."

"I know, Red. Thank you for not doing that, Red."

"Come on out and don't make noise. Something's wrong out there."

Horace grew just a bit more sober. "What do you mean?"

"I haven't seen Sean or Louis for quite a while. Maybe I've just missed them, us passing on opposite sides of buildings or something. But I think something's wrong."

Horace clambered out clumsily. "Don't talk so, Red. You scare me."

"You ought to be scared. When I saw you moving in this building I thought we had our man. I came in ready to shoot and almost did."

"I want to go back to my room."

"Come on. I'll take you."

They were almost out the door when they heard a

sound from the front end of the store. A mouse scurrying across a newspaper, maybe, or a breeze cutting an unusual angle around the trim of the building. Whatever it was, it was enough to make Red stop cold and raise his shotgun.

"Leave it be, Red! Let's get out!" Horace said in a fearful whisper.

"Hush."

"Just let it be!"

"Shhhh!"

Red bent over as if stalking and gripped his shotgun firmly. He crept toward the front of the store, peering about. Horace remained where he was until a big gust of wind rounded the building and shook the door in his face. He yelped and leapt back with remarkable grace, given his intoxication, and followed Red, preferring not to be alone.

"What is it, Red?"

"Keep quiet!"

"You see anything?"

"Blame it, Horace! Hush!"

Horace went no farther. He watched Red's slightly hunched form as he checked corners and probed beneath tables and behind partitions. At last Red turned, straightened, and shrugged.

"Just the wind, I suppose."

Horace wanted to tell him no, that it wasn't the wind, that a figure had emerged from the darkness behind him, but he couldn't even squeak, much less talk. He watched silently as Red stiffened and made a strange noise and dropped his shotgun. Red fell to his knees. He had been run through. Horace closed his eyes and thus heard but did not see the rest.

On Horace's gravestone, like Red's, they would put the words VICTIM OF MURDER. But for Horace that wouldn't be strictly accurate, for his heart already had stopped before the Gray Man with the long knife reached him.

When it was over and the bodies bore his identifying mark of mutilation, the Gray Man exited into the moon-light-mottled street, his blade flecking red onto the snow crust.

Chapter 11

Sleepless, Tellico lay on his bunk, his hands behind his head and his feet crossed. He looked unseeing at the low, shadowed ceiling. Images filled his mind.

A warm evening, dusky dark, with a drizzle of rain whispering on a canvas above. Thunder rumbled over leafless hills and gray lines angled down from the clouds to the gently rolling horizon.

A campfire struggled to burn in the clearing, and men in muddy boots, blue uniforms, and dark slickers moved about between the lines of canvas tents. Horses stirred about at a picket nearby, their smell pungent in the moist air.

Inside his tent a young chaplain knelt beside his cot and prayed. Oh God, give me an answer, for men die and I say words to them and feel unreal. Reopen my mind, Lord, to the understanding of your ways. Let me feel again the sense of your calling. Let me know the force that moves my life is you and the pattern of which I am a part is of your making.

Several nights now he had prayed like this, kneeling on the cold earth beneath his wet tent. But his answer had not yet come.

Since the war, everything had changed—including himself and the confidence he felt that God had called him to be a minister of the gospel. Upon joining the

Union army at the outbreak of hostilities, he had at first done his job with righteous zealotry. The Southern rebellion appalled him. Atrocities committed against unionists in the border states disgusted him. He deplored slavery, and rejected its oft-heard scriptural justifications. He went into the war convinced not that God was on the side of the Union, but that the Union was on the side of God.

He still believed the Union was right, but now seldom thought about it. His broad view of the war had become obscured by the narrower view of its effect on individual humans. He had seen too many torn bodies, watched too many young men die to care much anymore about big causes and national concerns.

The chaplain didn't think he could bear to kneel by another field hospital cot upon which writhed some bloody-fingered, wrist-gripping boy who had never dreamed he would not be home within a month of signing on, but now would not go home at all.

He became aware of someone in the tent doorway. He looked up, peculiarly ashamed he had been caught with his head bowed. He stood. "Come in, Private."

His visitor was a slender, slightly wan young man. He ducked through the slitted opening and came inside. He slipped off his cap.

"Reverend, may I speak to you?"

"Of course. What's your name, son?"

"Cottler. Private Darius Cottler."

"Have a seat, Darius."

The young man perched himself atop a folding stool. The chaplain sat on the side of his cot.

"How can I help you?"

The young man looked at his own feet. "I'm going to die tomorrow."

"I beg your pardon?"

"I'm going to die tomorrow. I've known it for about a week now."

The chaplain searched for something to say. "Darius, there's not a man here who doesn't dream about dying."

"This is no dream. I can't explain it. I just know."

From his mental file the chaplain tried to pull the proper ministerial response. He did not find it. He felt awkward in his silence, and the younger man sensed it.

"Don't worry over it, sir. I didn't come for comfort. And I'm not planning to run away. I came because I want to leave this with you."

He reached into his pocket and produced a medallion, smoothly worn, slightly battered. He held it out to the chaplain.

The medallion lay cool and heavy in the chaplain's hand. Engraved on the slick metal was the image of a river and a tree. He closed his fingers over it.

"What is this?"

"It's a thing left me by somebody I never got the chance to know. I hold it sometimes, and think about how things might have been if . . . well, if things had been different."

The chaplain was confused. "Is this some sort of family token?"

"Yes, in a way. At least for me."

"Why did you bring it to me?"

"Because when I die tomorrow I don't want some reb pulling it off me and throwing it away." He paused uncomfortably. "But it's not only that—I just want you to have it, you in particular. Maybe it's because you're a man of God."

Man of God. The words hit the chaplain in the pit of his stomach.

The private looked more troubled and spoke more hesitantly now. "Reverend, why does a man choose to become evil?"

It was a strange question, another the chaplain did not know how to answer. But he tried. "We're fallen beings, Darius. Darkness and light together. Sometimes we choose the darkness."

"But why? Why would a man choose to murder another one, or steal . . ." Here he hesitated. ". . . Or a father choose to desert his family and leave them nothing but a hell he created himself?"

The chaplain said, "I gather it's your family we're talking about here."

Darius Cottler nodded. For the next two hours he poured out the story of his life: desertion by his father even before his birth, the shame of bearing a family name ruined by the actions of a man he never even knew. Hearing it, the chaplain felt strangely humbled, ashamed of all the times he had complained about his lot, for young Cottler had seen much worse than he.

When he had told his story Darius and the chaplain prayed, Darius preparing himself for death. At length the young soldier rose, seeming now at peace. Outside the rain fell like hail, splattering the mud of the camp. The fire had surrendered to the downpour and now was just a steaming coalbed.

"God keep you, sir. We won't see each other again," Darius said.

The chaplain had the medallion in his palm. Darius looked at it and nodded. "I was right to give it to you. I think maybe there's a pattern to it all, even if we can't see it. Good-bye, sir." And he left.

That night the chaplain awakened to the crackle of thunder, wondering if he had merely dozed at his prayers and dreamed of the visit of Darius Cottler. But when he rolled in his cot the medallion lay on the trunk beside him.

The chaplain moved down a seemingly endless line of bodies covered with sheets soaked through with darkening blood. One by one he flipped them back, studying white faces, some with eyes tightly closed as if asleep, others with eyes wide open and scared, a few with no eyes at all.

These were old men and young, faces scarred and faces childlike. Some were freshly killed, others dead for days and horrible. Their stench was sickening; the chaplain held a handkerchief beneath his nose as he moved down the line.

Most were strangers, but several were men he had seen laughing and talking in the camps, or writing letters home or just sitting and staring as soldiers do before battle. A few were men who had sung and prayed in his services, or come to him in private for his counsel. God, did I help them? I don't feel like I helped them.

Then he turned another blanket and stopped. It was Darius Cottler. His face was white as bleached bone and unmarred, his lips and eyes closed.

The chaplain laid back the blanket and went off into the woods alone. That night he took a horse and rode away from camp.

Years now, yet the memory of Darius Cottler's dead face remained vivid. It haunted his thoughts, emerging at unlikely times, most often when he slept.

In the shack above Jerusalem Camp, Tellico rose and went to the stove. He opened the grate and added wood until flames rose and the room grew warm. He would get no sleep tonight, anyway; might as well have coffee.

He put the pot on to boil, went to the window, and looked out. No sign at the moment of the two who rode guard tonight; probably they were on the other side of town. He let the canvas curtain fall and turned away.

From the table he picked up the leatherbound portrait he had found in the snow. He hadn't yet shown it to Jared. Before he did he wanted to figure out what was so intriguing about it.

When the coffee was black and steaming he sat at his table and drank with slow sips, thinking back on the convoluted paths his life had followed since the night he had deserted.

He had never gone back to his home and congregation. He wrote a letter of resignation, then tore it up instead of sending it. Let them think he was dead.

He had ridden off with no aim in mind, crossing Missouri, meandering through many miles, months, and odd jobs, finally heading to Texas when the war was over.

He used his name at the beginning, but then one day someone asked him who he was and he gave a name he had once read on a map: Tellico. Why he did that he never figured out, but Tellico he remained from then on.

He worked as a hotel clerk, a line rider, a stage driver, even a barkeep. He slept in cheap rooms, bunkhouses, or beneath the stars.

Sometimes he would take out the medallion he now wore around his neck and look at it, thinking about the dead ivory face of Darius Cottler, and remembering the days God had been close and the pattern of life that Darius had mentioned had seemed apparent.

One night in a cheap hotel in Dallas, stirring on the

feather-leaking, flapjack-flat mattress, he heard the door open and saw Darius Cottler enter. The young man, phantasmic and pale, seemed to float six inches above the floor, and he said: *Consider that there may yet be a pattern to it all.*

Tellico threw the medallion at him, and it clattered against the wall and woke him up and he knew it all had been a dream.

He rode on soon after that, heading westward toward California as he followed a course that would inevitably lead to the snowbound Sierra town of Jerusalem Camp.

Chapter 12

Jared sat beside his father's sickbed, listening to his labored snoring, examining the lines of age marking his sallow face. He remembered when Isaiah's face had been young and strong; even now he could clearly picture his boyhood image of his father behind his pulpit, seeming ten feet tall as he boomed out the gospel like an angelic messenger. Jared had been in awe of his father throughout childhood; when Isaiah was in the pulpit he seemed to his young son like something between the earthly and the heavenly—flesh almost transformed to spirit. A magnificent but terrifying figure.

But he remembered as well the gentleness of that same face above him at night as he pulled the covers up beneath Jared's chin. And the short, beautiful prayer: "God, keep this son I love safe as he sleeps tonight."

Jared resettled himself for the hundredth time in the chair beside his father's bed. He drew tighter the blanket around his shoulders, his defense against the cold room.

"God," he whispered, "keep this father I love safe as he sleeps tonight."

He must have slept himself, for his next awareness was of his own sudden movement—catching himself from falling out of the chair—and then of his father's eyes upon him.

Jared recovered his senses, then smiled. Since Isaiah's collapse Jared always forced himself to smile when his father looked at him, for Doc Hull said it was important to keep his spirits and hopes as high as possible.

"How you feeling, Pa?"

"Better, I think," Isaiah said. "Much better."

The words roused emotion in Jared, for though they were mangled by Isaiah's partly paralyzed mouth, they were the first Isaiah had spoken since his collapse.

Jared went to the bedside and put his arms around his father.

"I love you, Pa."

Isaiah smiled as best he could.

Ingersoll heard the noise outside his window. He thought at first it was Belle Montgomery's old red hound, digging in the woodpile for dead mice, but the more he listened the less likely that seemed. It sounded more like somebody moving around.

"Loren?" he whispered.

Then he realized it might be the killer. He reached to his bedside table and picked up his Smith & Wesson. He went to his window and peered out through the slats of the shutters.

For a while he saw nothing unusual, but as he was about to turn away a patch of darkness moved at the edge of the forest. His eye caught it, lost it, caught it again. It was a vague image, better seen from the corner of his eye than straight on. It moved, stopped, darted, stopped again. . . .

A man. Ingersoll's breathing deepened, his hands began to sweat. "I got you, you murdering devil," he muttered. "It'll be Clyde Ingersoll who brings you down."

He put on his clothes in a clumsy rush and went to

the door. He stopped, trying to calm himself. His heart pumped beneath his shirt like the bellows down at the smithy when Jared Cable was pumping the fire to its hottest. Common sense tried to take over: I'm not up to this; I'm not young anymore. The time I shot down two highwaymen outside San Francisco is long past. But common sense faded when he again heard the stirring outside. There was a chance for glory here.

Ingersoll opened his door as quietly as he could and went outside. He paused on his porch, looking left and right. His knees felt as gelatinous as tree gum.

He headed left around the house. He tried to keep to the shadows, to move without noise, but he did an oafish job of it. By the time he reached the back of the house, he knew he must have been detected.

The clearing and adjacent dark woodland were utterly still, a frozen scene of snow and evergreens. Ingersoll pointed his shaking weapon here and there from a tense gunfighter stance. Cold and tension made his neck hurt.

But there was nothing there.

Relieved but also disappointed, he lowered his pistol and turned back toward his house.

He heard the faintest hint of movement. He wheeled, training his pistol toward the edge of the forest from where the noise had come.

There . . . someone moving. He almost fired, but didn't. It might be Rupert.

"Loren?" he said. He immediately wished he hadn't. Here he stood, exposed, and now he was deliberately drawing attention to himself. He felt foolish.

He had two options: return to the house or try to determine who was out there. The first was the most inviting, but pride wouldn't let him take it. So nervously he stepped toward the woods.

There, up ahead. Ingersoll dropped to one knee and leveled his pistol, but then the form was gone. He rose, beginning to feel the thrill of the chase. Whoever it was, he was running away. Old Clyde Ingersoll had the best of him. He pushed on.

Two, three more times the same thing happened: He spotted the figure, leveled on it, then lost it. He swore each time.

The woods yielded to another clearing. To the right stood the boot store and two of the town's oldest cabins, one now a storage shed, the other a chicken coop. Here Ingersoll stopped, having lost view of his prey.

He saw movement between the cabins. The man was crouched, apparently, for he moved low to the snowy ground. Ingersoll smiled. Try to skulk away from me, will you!

He rolled up his strength like a fist and unfurled it in a spurt of loping bounds to the narrow alley between the log structures. His bulky form scarcely fit in the space. "Hold it!" he commanded. "Not a move!"

Belle Montgomery's red hound yelped and ran off, leaving Ingersoll to slowly deflate in private humiliation.

"A dog!" he murmured. "I just chased down a dog!"

Disgusted, ashamed, grateful that no one had been about to see him, he slid the pistol beneath his belt and turned to go home.

He saw a face only inches before his own. His heart nearly exploded. He staggered back, mouth open, and fell to his knees.

The man, teeth flashing, leaned over Ingersoll. His long red hair dangled about his face like the strings of a dirty mop.

"Why ye trailing me, old man?"

Ingersoll searched vainly for his voice.

"I'll slit your throat right here! Why ye after me?"

"I . . . I . . ."

The other, though, apparently didn't expect an answer. His train of thought already had jumped to a new track. He asked, "Ye got money, old man?"

"No. No. But here . . . you can have my pistol."

"I will at that." The red-haired man disarmed Ingersoll.

"Now listen to me, old man. Ye didn't see me, ye didn't hear me, ye don't know a thing about me. Ye been in your bed asleep all night. Savvy?"

Ingersoll frantically nodded.

"Tell me something—there a man name of Tellico about this town?"

Ingersoll nodded again.

"Where?"

"In the old cabin on the hill across on the other side of town."

The man grinned. "Ye done good, old man."

He put his foot on Ingersoll's chest and pushed him into the snow. "Word gets out about me and I'll squash the entrails out of ye like the mush out of a beetle. You savvy that?"

"I won't talk."

"I'd kill ye except they'd miss ye and start looking. That's the only thing between ye and eternity, old man."

"Don't kill me. I won't talk."

"That's right, ye won't. Now git."

Ingersoll stood, so scared he could hardly keep his balance. He flailed along, thrashing clumsily in his fear, until he reached his house. He entered and slammed shut the door, bolted it, then fell onto the floor, shaking.

The red-haired man checked Ingersoll's Smith & Wesson. A good pistol, and a bonus for him, a souvenir to mark the night.

He began circling the town, searching for the

cabin where he would find Tellico. He did not see the gray figure who watched him from the darkness and then moved with no more noise than a whisper toward the flight of stairs leading to the second-level apartment of Claude and Matty Gregory above the dry goods store.

Tellico knew what he would find even before he rolled over the bodies of the dead sentinels. White faces with fearful expressions, thumbs chopped away from the right hands. Little warmth remained in the bodies. Whoever had done this could have been in town for some time now. He might have killed others already.

God, Tellico prayed, I've deserted you, but don't desert me. Especially not tonight.

He looked up to Jared's house. Should he rouse him? No. Not enough time. If Red Pringle still was walking guard in the middle of town he must be warned immediately.

Tellico loped as best the snow would let him down the slope toward Jerusalem Camp, wondering what kind of man it was who could surprise and kill two armed and mounted sentinels.

Jerusalem Camp was eerily beautiful here in the darkness. And eerily empty and still. Tellico entered the main street near the church, deliberately exposing himself so as not to surprise Red and risk getting shot. But as he moved through the town, he could not find Red.

Moments later he found Red's tracks in the snow, but that helped little, for Red had made many rounds and left tracks in all directions.

Tellico stood alone in the middle of town, trying to decide what to do.

Farther ahead a yellow spill of light moved across the snow. It came from Clyde Ingersoll's window; Ingersoll apparently was up and moving about inside with a lamp in his hand.

On impulse, Tellico headed to his door. Quietly, he knocked, then cupped his mouth against it and said, "Ingersoll—it's Tellico. Let me in!"

Ingersoll was a long time answering. When he did answer, the sight of him surprised Tellico: He was fully dressed, and the flickering kerosene flame from the smoking lamp in his hand illuminated the face of a man who apparently had been crying.

"Ingersoll, you all right?"

"God, Tellico, I'm glad you're alive. I was afraid I'd done you in."

"What are you talking about?"

Ingersoll pulled Tellico inside and bolted the door behind him. He shook like he had a fever.

Within a few minutes he had spilled out his story. When Tellico heard the description of the red-haired man he frowned.

"I'm lucky he didn't spot me," Tellico said. "He would have dropped me where I stood."

"Who is he, Tellico?"

"An old aquaintance who couldn't have come at a worse time. His name's Frank Coop. Ingersoll, listen to me. There's more dead men out there. Louis Brooks and Sean McFee—throats cut and thumbs gone. And I can't find Red Pringle anywhere."

Ingersoll started to cry. Tellico seized his wrist.

"Pull yourself together, Ingersoll. This is no time for it. We've got to sound an alarm. The church bell—I should have thought of that before. You got a weapon?"

"That man got it off me." Ingersoll hesitated. "He . . . uh . . . had to fight me for it."

"You're lucky he didn't cave in your skull. You got nothing else?"

"An old shotgun . . ."

"Get it."

Ingersoll went with his lamp to a wardrobe on the west side of the house. It was hung with musty-smelling clothes. He pushed them aside and from behind pulled out an old percussion-cap double barrel.

He raised the lamp to examine the rusted weapon, and the window beside him imploded, curtains bucking in and shredding as three slugs ripped through, two immediately snuffing out Ingersoll's life, the third blowing apart the lamp and scattering flaming liquid onto the clothes in the wardrobe.

Chapter 13

A grating laugh pierced in through the shattered window. The voice of Frank Coop said, "I got ye, Tellico!"

Tellico had dropped to the floor when the shots were fired. Now he rolled toward the door. The wardrobe already was engulfed in fire. The burning clothes inside it spewed choking black smoke.

"Are ye dead, Tellico?" Coop bellowed. "Or do ye need some more attention?"

Tellico pushed himself upright and burst out the door, cutting to the right. He made for a nearby barn. From the corner of his eye he saw his foe come around Ingersoll's smoking house, and heard him swear in disappointment at seeing him alive. Red flashes and loud gunfire blasts ruptured the snowy stillness.

Jared had jerked awake in his chair at the sound of the first shots. "What the—" He rushed to the window and looked toward the town, but he saw nothing out of the ordinary, except lights flickering on in a score of windows as others reacted to the gunfire.

By the time Jared had hefted up his galluses and found his coat, though, he saw something unusual: an orange glow on the far side of Jerusalem Camp.

He finished his rushed preparations. Anna appeared

at the door, a white madonna in a gown of pale flannel. Michael nestled against her hip. "Jared—"

"I got to go, Anna. There were gunshots, and something's burning. I'll be careful."

She was saying something else as he went out the door, but Jared did not hear it. He did not want to, for fear it would overcome his resolve.

He trotted and slid down the hill, and encountered the dead bodies of the two sentinels, their horses still loitering nearby. For several seconds he stared at the corpses.

The orange glow steadily grew brighter, casting light against the tops of the conifer forest beyond it and silhouetting the row of buildings between the fire and Jared. The conflagration appeared to be at or near Ingersoll's house. Jared hurried, dreading what he would find.

In the meantime, at the far edge of town, Tellico ducked behind a rain barrel at the rear of a building. The water at the top of the barrel was frozen and piled with snow that overhung the rim like the head on a beer. Coop appeared at the end of an alley. Two slugs slammed through the rain barrel, making water spew but missing Tellico.

Tellico rose and snapped off a shot that plowed a furrow at Coop's feet. Then he ran. He stopped when he reached the other side of the gingerbreaded, brightly painted dress shop. He put his back against the wall, panting, and slid down until he sat on his heels.

He heard voices in the street—others coming now, roused by the gunfire and the blaze that now sent vast tongues of flame skyward.

Coop rounded the rear of the dress shop; Tellico whipped the muzzle of his rifle toward him and fired. Coop grimaced and cursed and jumped back minus a little notch of flesh from his arm. Tellico ran into the street.

"Hey! Hey you!" somebody shouted.

Tellico assumed the yell was directed at him, but it wasn't. Coop had emerged into the street and been seen. But the shout made Coop pivot and go back the way he had come.

The shouter was Witt Essler. Armed with a big shotgun, he ran haltingly after Coop like a man chasing a grizzly he isn't sure he really wants to catch. Something moved somewhere to Witt's right. Panicking, Witt spun right on his heel and sent buckshot patterning through the night.

Jared felt pellets fan his cheek.

"Witt! Hold your fire! It's me!" he shouted.

Witt almost dropped his shotgun. "God, Jared, I'm sorry. . . ."

Gunsmith Curly Malone and a handful of other men appeared and converged in the middle of the street. Others rushed toward Ingersoll's burning house, scrambling for buckets, breaking the ice on rain barrels, and raising a babble of voices. Witt was shaking, still apologizing to Jared. Conversation for the next few moments came in a rush:

"Louis and Sean are dead," Jared said. "Has anybody seen Red Pringle?"

Witt said, "I didn't see Red. But I saw a red-haired man I never saw before taking after your deputy with a gun."

"After Tellico? Where is he?"

"I don't know. He headed yonder."

"What about the red-haired fellow?"

Witt pointed at the alley beside the dress shop.

Curly was looking at the fiery shell of Ingersoll's house. "Almighty God—is Clyde still in there?"

Suddenly, Witt pointed again at the alley and shouted a warning. Several shots popped. Jared felt like somebody had rammed a hot knife through the fleshy part of his upper arm. He was hit with enough force to knock him down. The men scattered.

In the alley Tellico fired again at Frank Coop. During the confusion Tellico had recrossed the street and surprised Coop where he hid. Coop fired on him, Tellico fired back. The shot that had struck Jared was just a wild stray.

Tellico saw Jared fall and immediately forgot Coop, who took the chance to dart to the forest. Tellico came to Jared's side, picked him up by the left arm, and dragged him to the street. He gave Jared's bleeding shoulder a cursory inspection.

"Get Doc Hull," he ordered Witt.

"It's nothing," Jared protested. "Go after that man!" Then he fainted.

Tellico and Curly together hefted Jared to his feet, taking care not to stress the wound.

"Let's take him to my shop," Curly volunteered. "I've got some liquor hid in there we can clean the wound with."

Witt waved at Ingersoll's house, now thoroughly involved with the fire. "What about Clyde?"

"He's dead," Tellico said.

Claude Gregory looked into the snakeskin whiteness of a pitted face framed by a tangle of matted hair. The Gray Man drew back his lips and showed a row of broken yellow through a mustache that overhung his mouth.

"It's been many a year since I saw you last, Claude Gregory. Oh yes, I know you. And you know me, too."

"Please," Claude pleaded. "Do what you want to me, but let her go. She's done you no harm."

The Gray Man turned his yellow smile down upon the elderly woman struggling in his arms. "Indeed. Why should any man harm the loved one of another?"

"Damn you!" Claude whispered hoarsely. "Crawl back into hell and leave us alone!"

"It's hell indeed I came from, and soon enough I'll return. And I will have company."

Tears brimmed in Claude's eyes.

The old man looked at him with contempt. "You think you can move me with tears? Who saw *my* tears when I tore at dirt and rocks until my fingers were eaten away? Did you cry for me or for the son you took from me? Did you?"

Claude sobbed. "In the name of God, let my wife go!"

The Gray Man kept talking. "How many times have you lain awake at night, Claude Gregory, trying to forget what you did? I haven't forgotten."

"Please, let her go."

The Gray Man laughed. Matty struggled uselessly. The grime-caked face drew near to hers.

"Just how well do you know your husband, my dear? Has he ever told you about his little trip to Carolina thirty-five years ago?"

"Claude, make him let me go!"

Claude put his hands over his eyes.

"Perhaps I should tell you, if he hasn't. About this fine Christian gentleman who tried to cover his sin with shovels of dirt and years of silence. Do you want to tell her, Claude, or shall I?"

Claude suddenly grew angry and went at his tormentor.

The Gray Man flung Matty aside. Her head struck the corner of a cabinet and she collapsed. Claude wrapped his fingers around the old man's throat and began to squeeze. Suddenly he stopped. He staggered backward, blood streaming from a shallow stab wound above his stomach.

The Gray Man brought up his long knife again.

But then the noise of gunfire came up from the street below. The Gray Man went to the window and peered out. Claude, fighting to keep his senses, tried with his hand to stanch the flow of his blood. The unsteady light of Ingersoll's flaming house detailed the angular profile of the old man at the window.

The man dropped the curtain and turned. Claude was crawling to his wife's still form. The Gray Man went to him and kicked him over. Claude lost consciousness.

The Gray Man knelt and stretched out Claude's right hand and brought out his knife again.

When he was done he spilled coal oil on the Gregorys' threadbare old couch. He removed the globe of a lamp and cranked the wick high. "For my son," he said, as he tossed the flaming lamp onto the couch.

He opened the door quietly, and with great stealth slipped back into the night, making for the forest.

Anna Cable heard the rattle of the latch and looked up in both anticipation and dread. The door swung open; Jared was there. His arm was bloodied and bandaged. "Don't fret, I'm all right," he said. "Just a scratch."

She went to him, put her arms around him, and kissed him.

"I've got coffee waiting for you, honey," she said. "Come in and sit down."

"Where's Michael?"

"Asleep in the chair beside Isaiah."

"Is Pa all right?"

"Sleeping, too. Here—sit." She put the coffee in his hand.

For several minutes Jared let the hot drink put life back into him and calm him.

"We saw him tonight, Anna."

"Saw who?"

"The killer. A red-haired fellow." He took another sip. "Tellico almost got him."

"Almost," Anna said, disappointed.

Jared smiled and touched her hand. "I love you. Couldn't make it without you."

"You don't have to."

Jared lowered his head. "It's hell down there, Anna. Five people are dead."

Anna gazed at him in horror. He continued. "Sean McFee. Louis Brooks. Red Pringle. Horace Bailer. Poor old Clyde Ingersoll. And Matty and Claude—he burned their place around them. We barely got them out, both of them unconscious. They may not make it yet. Claude had been stabbed. And his thumb . . ." Jared's eyes misted. "Clyde wasn't so lucky. There's nothing left of him at all. Horrible."

"How could one man kill five people?"

"Maybe he's more than a man. Maybe he's a demon."

"You have to get some sleep, honey."

"I can't. I'd just feel worse."

Anna hugged him. "I'll fix you something to eat." She went to the stove and stirred the fire.

Below, at the far edge of town, Tellico stood beside the black shell of Ingersoll's house. He sought out the place where Ingersoll had fallen. My fault he's dead. Coop was trying to kill me. My fault—and my responsibility to do something about it.

Chapter 14

Jared, trailed by a dozen men, picked his way up the steep incline of the snowy mountain. He was weary from his restless night, and his eyes blazed angrily.

Tellico should be here. But he wasn't. Not a trace of him. He had run out when things were at their worst.

Jared was ashamed he had trusted him so.

He couldn't dwell on that now. Had a job to do. An overwhelming sense of unreality hung over this whole amazing affair. Five dead in one night! And three well armed when it happened. What kind of enemy did they face here?

Witt touched Jared's shoulder. The wind howled so loudly Witt had to shout at him.

"Wind's blown over all the tracks!"

Witt was right. They had been moving blindly ahead with little to guide them. The wind whipped the dry snow into shifting drifts, hiding real trails, creating false ones.

"So what do you suggest?" Jared yelled back through the bitter howling.

Witt shrugged. "Head back?"

"No. Keep moving. Maybe higher up we'll see something."

Witt looked skeptical, but Jared wouldn't stop. To

him, just trying was better than sitting down there in that fear-ridden town, dreading the approach of another night.

So they continued up the slope. The wind screamed like a demon.

Elsewhere in the mountains, Tellico was as frustrated as Jared. He seriously pondered climbing up on some rock or deadfallen tree and yelling as loudly as he could for Frank Coop. He hated this impossible cat-and-mousing. Coop probably was three miles away from here by now. Coop was tenacious, certainly—that he had trailed Tellico as far as Jerusalem Camp proved that. But he wasn't foolish.

You've probably written me off by now, Frank Coop, but I've not written you off. You're trapped in this valley like the rest of us, whether you know it yet or not. I'll find you.

The defiant thoughts felt good but meant little unless he could find Coop quickly. Before dark he would have to return to Jerusalem Camp. At the moment the town needed every man.

Frank Coop. The very thought of the man took Tellico back to his first encounter with the red-haired devil.

That had been in Placerville. It was the end of an autumn day. Tellico rode in on his bay mare. He was hungry and very thirsty.

He saw a stark little outpost ahead, surrounded by a pinepole fence and a pack of mangy strays. Several horses were tethered out front; from inside the light-spilling interior, loud laughter and shouts echoed out into the dusk. A saloon. He didn't think much of saloons, but he was thirsty enough to overlook that for the moment.

He tethered up beside the other horses and went to the door. The clamor inside grew louder. He pushed open the door.

Unexpectedly, the saloon grew quiet as a funeral parlor. The dozen men inside turned to him with odd expressions on their faces.

Tellico stood stock-still in the doorway, wondering what he had walked into. Then from the midst of the group erupted the shrill cry of a woman: "Mother of God, help me!"

One of the men cocked his head and looked at Tellico like he was trying to peer through his insides. "Having us a little party," he said. "Kind of private."

"Where's the lady?" Tellico asked.

The man misinterpreted Tellico's intent, for he relaxed and grinned broadly. "If you're patient you'll get a turn too."

The group shifted, and what Tellico saw revolted him. A young Mexican lady cowered on the floor against the far wall, clinging to her torn clothing. Her lip bled and she looked pleadingly at Tellico.

Tellico felt like someone had just clubbed him in the gut.

The noise began anew as a big man with hair the color of fire moved toward the girl. His grizzly-paw hand swept down and roughly grasped her wrist.

"C'mon, honey. C'mon now," he said. "Old Frank Coop's nice to girls that are nice to him."

Tellico felt locked to the floor, but the floor seemed to be rocking. The girl looked at him again, imploring his help, but he remained still.

The red-haired man pulled her to her feet and wrapped his arms crushingly around her. His broad face went to hers, and he kissed her. His long red hair strung down over her cheeks.

The girl pushed him back and spat like she had ingested a roach.

Coop's smile died. He cursed, then brought up his hand and slapped her. The blow threw her against the wall, where she collapsed, stunned. Coop went toward her.

Tellico fired a shot through the ceiling. Again the place went quiet and every man turned to him. He was as surprised as any of them, for he had done it almost automatically.

"Put that away," somebody said. "Wait your turn like the rest."

Tellico waved the pistol across the group. "Against the wall, hands up," he said. "Ma'am, you come with me."

The girl ran to him, past him, out the door. "Mine's the bay mare," he called to her without looking away from the men. "Unhitch her and mount up. I'll be out directly."

"We'll swing you from a tree," somebody said. Another man slipped a hand beneath his coat. Tellico shot him through the knee.

"If anybody else moves, it's his judgment day," Tellico said. "When I get outside I'll be watching. So much as a face at the window and I'll put a hole through it."

Tellico backed away to the door. But suddenly the girl came back inside, and this time she had Tellico's saddle rifle.

"No!" Tellico shouted in tandem with the first blast.

Men screamed. One fell, then another. The shots continued, the girl yelling with every shot. It became a scene out of hell: men falling, blood on the floor, screams of agony and panic.

Somehow Tellico got her outside again, and on the horse. He freed and spooked the other mounts there, then mounted in front of her. The bay mare ran clumsily because of the loose shoe, but it ran well. When night came they were far from Placerville. The girl was asleep beneath Tellico's blanket and Tellico himself sat on the edge of a bluff, hidden in brush, watching the road below where riders searched unrelentingly.

One of them was Frank Coop.

Her name was Maria Alvarado, and in the light of morning Tellico saw eyes surprisingly different than those of the crying victim in the saloon. These were as cold as any he had ever seen before, and hard as marble.

She asked him who he was and why he had helped her, and he tried to explain. When he told her he had been a preacher, she laughed.

"You, señor, are a preacher? Well, for money I will make you a very happy preacher, no?"

Tellico merely looked at her.

She laughed again. "You are shocked at me? You sell holy words. I sell myself."

"Is that why you were in the saloon? It was not a rape?"

"Oh yes, it was rape. That happens sometimes to us. But I thought they would kill me this time. That is why I was afraid and angry. That is why I shot them."

Tellico turned away. *God in heaven, what have I gotten into?* Maria Alvarado had used his rifle—his rifle—to wound and probably kill several men. He himself had wounded one. There wasn't a court in the land that wouldn't hang him. He was at the least an accessory to murder.

They rode overland, through the mountains, and so escaped capture. Maria seemed to feel no remorse at what had happened, or any fear of its consequences. She offered herself to Tellico again and again, laughing when he spurned her. It was a tremendous joke to her until the final time, when he became angry and shoved her to the ground. She burst into tears and ran away.

The next night she stole his rifle and food and walked away. When Tellico found she was gone he was joyous. Let her have the rifle and the supplies; it was worth it to be rid of her. He was just glad she hadn't stolen the bay. She probably would have, if she could have done it without awakening him.

He rode to San Francisco and found a job cleaning and maintaining a store building with two attorneys' offices overhead. From one of the office windows, as he cleaned one night, he saw Coop ride in with two other men. They were so close he could hear their loud talk through the open window. Coop called one of them Mansell, the other Joe.

The next day he did not see them and hoped they were gone, but then word came back to him that they were asking around for someone of his description. Tellico thought about running, but pride and lack of resources wouldn't allow it. One night shortly after, he encountered Coop in the street. Coop reached first but Tellico somehow got off the first shot. Coop did not stay to battle; he turned and ran.

Tellico ran too, hiding elsewhere in the city. The next morning he sought out a church and attended the service, drinking in every hymn and word, stumbling to the altar when it was through and crying out a prayer. He walked out feeling better, cleaner.

But at dusk he saw Coop on the veranda of a brothel with a fat woman on his knee, so heavily painted she looked cadaverous. When Coop saw him he pushed the woman aside and came after him, shooting into the thickening darkness as Tellico ran. "I'm going to find ye and kill ye, Tellico," the bearded man shouted. "Hunt ye down like a varmit and skin ye alive."

Monday morning Tellico saddled the bay mare and rode out toward the Sierras, toward a little mining town called Jerusalem Camp. It was a place, he had once heard, where people worshiped God and a man could lose himself.

It did not take long to realize he was being followed. Frank Coop's threat, it appeared, was not idle. He and his partners really wanted him dead. Tellico had to outrun them.

So he had pushed on toward Jerusalem Camp as the first blizzard of winter blasted the Sierras.

Chapter 15

"Tellico."

The speaker was Coop, but Tellico hardly recognized his voice, for he had spoken softly and not in his usual harsh bellow. Tellico whirled to face Coop, who pointed a pistol at him from behind a boulder where he had been hiding.

"I could have picked ye off five minutes ago, but it's better to look ye in the face," Coop said. "And besides, I wanted to tell ye something."

Tellico asked, "How'd you find out my name?"

"That's just what I wanted to tell ye. The girl, she sang it out quick enough when we caught her. She won't sing no more." He smiled, letting the implication sink in. "Ye and her killed two of my oldest friends, Tellico, and in Frisco ye just made it worse. I ain't a man who forgets."

"I didn't kill anybody. I wounded one man."

"Ye killed, she killed, it don't matter. Ye did it together and I blame ye both."

Tellico wondered what Maria Alvarado had suffered at this man's hands before she died. He prayed for her soul.

"Drop your weapons, Tellico."

Rage boiled over. "No," Tellico said. Ignoring the risk, he swung down his rifle and fired off a shot, but the slug whined past Coop's head high into the mountain air. Coop fired his pistol. Tellico yelled at the impact of the bullet. It was like being pounded across the upper chest with a club. His feet kicked out and he fell on his back in the snow. The men were at the top of a steep slope, and Tellico rolled down it, staining the snow red as he went. Coop's laugh became indistinct and more distant, muffled through a ringing in his ears.

Tellico slowly rose and examined himself. The bullet had entered low on his right shoulder. The wound hurt terribly, a pulsing kind of hurt that radiated out in waves from the bleeding hole.

He became dizzy and fell again, flopping across the top of a rounded boulder. Half conscious, he lazily slid down the other side, unable to stop himself, even when he saw there was nothing beyond the boulder but emptiness. He squeezed his eyes shut as he pitched into the air and fell about fifteen feet onto a huge, slanted rock face. He slid down it at a cross angle, and when he reached the bottom he was senseless.

His next awareness seemed to be a dream: He was dead, yet alive, too, and squeezed into a coffin far too small. It constricted his chest, squeezing tighter when he moved. It threatened to crack his ribs. Every breath came hard and painfully.

The dream gave way to reality, but reality was no improvement. He had reached the bottom of the sloping rock and was trapped firmly between it and a similar rock face that sloped down opposite it, forming a natural funnel. His own weight worked against him. He tried to move, but each time he only slid down a little farther. He had landed on his right side and his right arm dangled below him, touching nothing. He realized that he might not be at the true bottom of the funnel at all, that this tight hole might open into some dark Sierra cavern. He would never be found. His corpse would lie there, to rot and be eaten by worms and blind, crusty subterranean things. He could picture the foul, decaying thing that used to be himself, lost in ceaseless night.

He seized control of his mind at the last moment before panic. Think, Tellico. Don't give in. Figure out what you have to do and do it.

He evaluated his position. He could move a bit, though it hurt badly and seemed only to put him in more danger. His wounded shoulder ached horribly, but was wedged tightly against the rock and thus was not bleeding much. That was good, but that was about it.

He shifted his eyes to the left and looked up. The sloping rock face seemed endless; beyond its gentle camber the sky was an even gray. Much darker than before.

Night was coming. Tellico fought despair. His consciousness, mercifully, rolled away like a loose stone and so he did not have to watch daylight fade and darkness fall.

Where he was he did not know. He seemed to be floating in warm liquid, or hovering in the sky on a summer night. He felt no pain, just a strong sense of well-being. He opened his eyes.

He saw bursts of color spreading before him in no clear pattern. They moved and swirled, coming together to form images from his memory, lasting no longer than the faces one sees in the leaping flames on a hearth.

Tellico heard his own voice: Out of the depths have I cried unto thee, O Lord. Lord, hear my voice, let thine ears be attentive to the voice of my supplications.

Then something warm and furred brushed against his right hand and the dream became confused. When it happened again the dream vanished.

He opened his eyes as he felt a new stab of pain in

his wounded chest. Then, once again, a brushing, bristly something moving against the hand that dangled into the open space below the wedged rocks.

He curled his fingers, feeling helpless. Some beast down there—and any moment it would sink long teeth into his hand. . . .

A happier realization came. If there was an animal moving down there, then there was a surface not far below. Hope arose. He squeezed his eyes closed. *Out of the depths have I cried unto thee, O Lord. . . .*

He steeled himself and wrenched his body as powerfully as he could. He scraped between stones, yelled in pain, and fell hard against a smooth rock surface no more than five feet below.

Coop had long since given up on finding Tellico. He had seen him roll and fall out of view, but try though he did, he could not find him. Well, he must be dead. Couldn't have survived both a bullet and a fall like that. Job completed. Coop congratulated himself.

Now that night had come, Coop wished he was out of these mountains. It was mighty cold up here, and lonesome. Nothing to eat but a little hardtack. He wondered what had happened to Mansell and Joe. He hoped they had frozen to death, the lousy deserters. Mansell always had taken his poker too seriously. Losing a couple of games was no reason to split up their partnership and run out. He'd even taken Joe with him. And Coop sick and holed up in that deserted cabin.

He chewed his hardtack and huddled close to the small, smokeless fire he had built in a rock depression. It was barely enough to keep off the chill. He considered building a bigger one, but it could be that somebody from the town was still about in the mountains, unlikely though that seemed. Still, he had stirred up quite a ruckus in Jerusalem Camp. Watching the town after he escaped it the night before, it had appeared that more than one building had burned down. Probably spread from the fire in that house where he had shot at Tellico. Coop grinned, proud of himself.

He nodded and dozed until the fire burned low and the cold got to him. He blinked awake and rose with his blankets still around him to get more wood. He stopped, bewildered.

Across from him on the other side of the bed of embers he saw what appeared to be a mound of snow that, strangely, had not been there before. Maybe heat from the fire had melted loose some accumulation from a tree above. Yet now that he looked more closely it looked less like snow.

And it wasn't. It was a man wrapped in a gray-white fur cloak. He was looking down.

Coop danced back three steps in surprise.

"Who ye be? Why ye sneak into a man's camp?"

The man who was huddled beneath the fur cloak slowly lifted his head. Coop saw the glitter of two dark eyes. The man's form was hard to delineate in the darkness; he seemed part of the very mountain.

Coop spouted a threat, but with less bluster now that he had seen the unnerving eyes. "I ought to blow off your head, old man." He reached for his pistol and found the holster empty. The old man must have slipped out the pistol while he slept. He looked aghast at his tormentor, realizing that he was being toyed with like a mouse between a cat's paws.

Frank Coop screamed in tandem with the blast of the long Henry rifle whose muzzle suddenly prodded out from beneath the folds of the fur robe. The slug shot past him.

He turned and ran.

* * *

"I'm worn out," Witt Essler said to his wife. "Jared wouldn't give up the chase. We kept on long after we had lost all our sign."

Deb Essler gave him a terrible look. "Dead men in the streets. Thumbs sliced off corpses. Fires set to burn up old people. It's horrible. I can't understand why it's happening."

Witt didn't offer any answers. He was no philosopher and spent little time trying to figure out the whys of life. The whats were enough for him.

"I wonder what became of Tellico?" he said. "Jared thinks he cut out. Deserted after what happened last night."

"Good. I hope he has. This town has been a place of misery since he came. It's his fault," Deb said.

"Now Deb. You know he wasn't involved in the killing. It has to be that red-haired fellow I saw."

"And who did you say he was after? Tellico. Tellico may not be the killer, but he's the one who attracted him to Jerusalem Camp!"

Witt hadn't thought of it like that. His wife's words made some sense. Still, he wasn't ready to give up on Tellico.

"I don't believe Tellico cut out," he said. "I think he's out there in those mountains still looking for the killer."

"In the dark? No. He's gone. I hope he buries himself in an avalanche trying to go through the pass."

"Deb! You talk such terrible ways these days."

"These are terrible times. And this is a terrible town, Witt. I want to leave it in the spring. I don't want to live here anymore."

Witt patted her arm. "Honey, when we catch old Mister Red Hair you'll feel different."

"Pa?"

Witt and Deb jumped. They hadn't heard Jimmy slip into the room.

"The killer don't have red hair. Geoffrey Davithon thaw him at hith window before he killed anybody, and he had a long gray beard. No red hair."

Witt briefly thought about it, then waved it off. "You boys ought not talk silly truck like that," Witt said. "Geoffrey's had enough trouble without making up spooks with gray hair."

"He didn't make it up, I thwear! Lee Weller, he theen him too, looking at him from the edge of the woodth."

"Geoffrey Davison, Lee Weller . . . boy, you can't take the word of just anybody. I saw the man, and his hair was red as a woodpecker crest. And what are you doing up, anyway? You're supposed to be in bed."

"Can't thleep, Pa."

Witt smiled sympathetically. "Nobody's sleeping much these nights, son. Want to crawl in with us?"

Jimmy grinned, showing his gappy teeth. He climbed in between his mother and father, and was the only soul in Jerusalem Camp who felt utterly safe.

Chapter 16

Jared Cable came to his father's bedside.

"How you feeling, Pa?"

"A little stronger," the old preacher said in his twisted voice.

"I'm glad."

Isaiah said, "There's been more killed, I heard."

Jared's brows lowered. "Who's been talking to you? Michael?"

Isaiah nodded.

Jared glared. "I'll have a word with that boy, then. You weren't supposed to be told anything to worry you."

"Well, now I know. Tell me what happened."

Jared outlined what had occurred and who had died. Telling him about the near-murder of Claude and Matty was the hardest part. "The worst of it is he cut off Claude's thumb. He left Matty alone, thank God."

Isaiah closed his eyes.

Jared went on, "We went looking for the killer's trail but we had no luck. He's still out there."

The father and son sat quietly for a while. Finally Isaiah said, "Jared, do you really understand that all men are sinners?"

Jared was puzzled. "Sure I do."

"I mean all men. Me included."

Jared nodded, wondering what his father was driving at.

"There are things a man does in his life—bad things he didn't want to do. Maybe he might think they're long forgotten, when they really aren't."

Isaiah was frightened by his father's seemingly directionless babbling. He wondered if the apoplexy had taken his mind.

Isaiah kept on. "Jared, it may be that soon you'll hear some things that you don't want to hear about me. All I want to know is that you'll love me just the same, and won't look down on me."

Now his voice began to rise and become choked with emotion. Isaiah gripped Jared's arm.

"You've got to understand, Jared, we didn't mean to do it. Nobody meant for it to happen. We were scared to death, that's all."

Jared could stand this no longer. He rose, pulling free from his father's clawing grip. The sallow hand fell back onto the sheets.

"You're getting all worked up and not making any sense. I don't know what you're talking about, and you don't either. You need to rest," Jared said.

Isaiah wiped his eyes. "We just didn't know what to do. We didn't mean for anything bad to happen."

"You're tired, Pa. Settle down. Sleep." He searched for something encouraging to say. "We'll have our killer caught soon enough. Witt Essler saw him—a fellow maybe close to forty. We'll catch up with him."

Isaiah appeared confused. "Forty?"

"Yes. You go on to sleep, now."

Jared walked out.

He closed the bedroom door gently. Alone, Isaiah looked to the ceiling and closed his eyes.

"Forty . . . then it isn't him after all," he said. A chuckle rose from deep within. "Praise Jehovah, it isn't him at all!"

Tellico could hardly breathe. The musky scent of fur and droppings hung thick in the atmosphere of this tight little cavern. He pushed up on his elbows and groaned. He had fallen directly on his wounded shoulder and blood flowed freely from it. It hurt like the devil.

He froze when he heard a growl nearby. In this black hole he could see nothing, but he had an immediate mental image of a dripping muzzle, cruel red eyes, a pink, hungry mouth. . . .

"Easy, easy," he said. His hand slid back to his pocket and dug out a box of sulfur matches. "You don't want me, Ephraim. You'll break a tooth on me. . . ."

He struck a match. It flared brightly for a moment before a burst of wind through the cave snuffed it. Tellico lowered his head in the darkness and sighed in relief.

Just a cub. More scared than he was.

He felt the wind again, and began crawling in the direction from which it blew.

The cub growled and squeaked and backed away, and Tellico made it out.

The night sky was half-covered with clouds; they lay like a gray beach against an ocean of velvet on which stars sailed. The moonlight delineated the serrated line of mountaintops against the backdrop of night. A vast and snowy desolation, wildly beautiful, but tonight seeming utterly alien and hostile.

Tellico found a recess, built a small fire, and let it burn to embers. He dug out a depression with his heel and kicked the coals into it, then covered them with dirt. He squatted Indian-style, with his legs circling the mound, and threw his coat around him like a robe to hold in the heat.

Lord, my shoulder hurts. Worse by the minute, and now I feel like I've got a fever. Let me make it until morning, and get me back to Jerusalem Camp.

He fell asleep and dreamed of the war and Darius Cottler.

How the old man had missed at that range Frank Coop didn't know, but he wasn't about to question providence. He had made it away with not a scratch. The bullet had whizzed past and he had turned on his heels and run.

When morning came, Coop struggled without his snowshoes through snow that reached his thighs. He came to the edge of the forest and waded into a snowfield, feeling very exposed. He continually looked over his shoulder, imagining he could feel the old man up there in the rocks, watching him, maybe drawing a bead on him.

Jerusalem Camp lay to the southeast. Coop pictured its warm houses, fireplaces, food . . . but Jerusalem Camp could never be an option for him. He pushed on.

He had in mind the deserted cabin in which he had been laid up sick when Mansell and Joe had deserted him—and where he similarly had deserted that battered-up old codger with the skis and busted ribs. The varmit would be dead by now, stinking up the place like a rat in a long-sprung trap. Oh well, maybe he would be frozen and not too rank. Coop could get rid of him, build a fire, snare a rabbit, and have a hot meal.

On the other side of the snowfield he found a ridge of rock from which the snow had blown clean. He climbed upon it and traveled much faster without leaving tracks. As the morning gave way to a cold noon, he reached and went through a familiar little pass. He saw the cabin.

Smoke poured from the chimney.

Amazed, he paused. That old fellow couldn't still be alive. Must be somebody else. A hunter, maybe . . . or the bearded fellow who had shot at him. No. Couldn't be. He couldn't have reached here that quickly.

Well, whoever it was would have to share that fire and whatever victuals he might have. Coop was almost frozen through, and he'd be hanged before he'd shiver outside when he could be warm by that hearth.

He crept as cautiously and covertly as his numb legs would allow him toward the cabin, wishing he were armed.

Tellico awakened feeling very ill. His wounded shoulder was swollen. When he stood he was dizzy and doubled over in dry heaves.

He realized he had to make it back to Jerusalem Camp soon or die. A fever would kill a man fast in the cold mountains. He forced himself to begin walking.

He either had to climb or circle the ridge to have any hope of reaching the town without getting lost. He was too weak to climb, so circle it would be.

He found a stout stick and used it like a crutch and balance pole. He wondered where Coop was, and if he was still looking for him.

Tellico felt too sick to care. He wondered if his wound was putrefying. He thought about looking at it, but decided against it. It would only make things worse.

He traveled through the morning and into the afternoon, stumbling along. His lack of snowshoes made progress difficult. He stopped for a few minutes to catch his breath, longing for rest. . . .

Cold against his face woke him up. He had fainted and fallen prone in the snow. Fear pulsed through him. He realized how dangerous his situation was.

He went on, even though he hardly had the strength to move.

The mountains and snow confused him. Too hurt and fevered to think, he wandered far off the course to Jerusalem Camp. He was unbearably cold.

Finally he saw a cabin ahead of him. It was occupied, for the chimney smoked and the window was a square of light. He descended to it, and collapsed at the door.

Someone moved inside. The door opened, and Loren Rupert looked down at him. Tellico figured he was dreaming. Dream or not, he crawled inside.

Tellico made it to the hearth and sank to the floor, bathing in heat. He let it drive the chill from him. He turned to Rupert, who was still there, looking too solid and tangible to be a hallucination.

Then he saw something on the floor. Frank Coop —dead. I'm seeing things after all, he thought blankly before he passed out.

Chapter 17

"It was amazing," Witt said to the men grouped around the woodstove. "There we were, just gone out to ride guard, when we saw them. Staggering in out of the woods. We almost shot them before we recognized them."

"Is it true Rupert was carrying Tellico?" asked a listener.

"Both carrying each other is more like it. Both in a bad way. Tellico's laid up in his cabin, still crazy with fever. Has a putrefied bullet wound. Rupert's doing better, and talking a mile a minute. I think he's right proud of being the one who did in the killer, even if it was an accident."

Witt outlined Rupert's story—how he had fallen and hurt himself, but had made it to a cabin where he found the red-haired man. The man had tortured him, asking for money and for information about Tellico's whereabouts, then had left him to die. But Rupert had found some canned food stashed in a cache beneath a floorboard, apparently there for years. He broke the rusty cans open with rocks, and on that food he had survived until the red-haired man unexpectedly showed up again, minus his weapons and the snowshoes he had stolen from Rupert. When he made a violent move toward Rupert,

Rupert had picked up a heavy stick of firewood and swung at him. The move reinjured Rupert's ribs, but the red-haired man had fallen back and hit his head on the stone hearth, and from then on hadn't moved. Shortly afterward, Tellico also had appeared at the cabin door, in bad shape. Rupert, despite his own injuries, had nursed him as best he could and together they had made it back to Jerusalem Camp.

News of the death of the red-haired man brought elation to the town.

"But what I can't figure," Witt said, "is why this bird did what he did. It appears he was after Tellico—but why did he kill the Davisons, or Sean McFee, or any of them? And remember, the Davisons were killed before Tellico ever came to town. Some of it doesn't make sense. But one thing is clear: It was Tellico who drew the killer here. In a way that makes it his fault. I'll be anxious to hear what he has to say for himself once he's back on his feet."

Isaiah was much improved these past two days, and for that Jared was very grateful. The preacher was sitting up, talking, even walking about—and his speech was better. He also ate a lot more than before.

Jared attributed the improvement to the good news Rupert had brought back. The killer was dead; the threat was over.

For Jared it was a lifted burden. The only thing that bothered him was that the killer apparently was linked to Tellico. And Jared still did not understand Tellico's recent absence. Had he trailed the killer, or merely run away and encountered him by accident? Until Tellico was over his fever he would not know.

Jared pondered questions such as this as he carried

his father's midday meal to him on a steaming plate. He sat back and watched the old man satisfy his renewed appetite.

"Pa, what was that you said about the past and sin and all that?" Jared asked.

"Forget about it," Isaiah said. "It meant nothing."

Later, Jared headed up the hill toward Tellico's shack, where a couple of the town's men guarded him. Jared hadn't ordered it; the men of the town had taken the job on themselves. Jared found disturbing the amount of venom directed against Tellico now that he was perceived as being the one who had—at least indirectly—brought the Killing Winter to Jerusalem Camp.

"How is he?" Jared asked.

"Back among the living," one of them said. "His fever broke."

Tellico nodded a greeting when Jared entered.

"How you feeling?"

"Like I've been run over by a wagon." He rubbed his wounded shoulder. "I understand I've gone from deputy to prisoner again."

"Well, it seems pretty evident to folks that you attracted the killer to Jerusalem Camp."

Tellico scratched his thickening beard. "Frank Coop. He was after me, that I can't deny. He blamed me for the deaths of some friends, though it wasn't me who killed them. No need to go into all that, though. The important thing is that Frank Coop wasn't the killer."

"Not the killer? He shot Ingersoll, didn't he?"

"He did, thinking it was me, because I had gone inside Ingersoll's house just a few moments before. But he didn't kill any of the others."

Jared, eager like the rest of the town to believe the

threat was past, did not like what he was hearing. "How can you be sure?"

"Because I know who the real killer is. Let me show you."

Tellico reached beneath his shirt and removed the medallion.

"I got this during the war," he said. "A young soldier named Darius Cottler gave it to me the night before he was killed. It was a memento of his father, who deserted his mother before Darius was born. That wasn't enough to keep the father's reputation from ruining the lives of Darius and his family, though. The boy told me all about it. Darius's father was a wicked man. Maybe insane, maybe just evil. He did some terrible things. There was talk that he had killed some people. There was an older Cottler son, too, who people said was almost as bad as the father. Darius never knew him, either.

"When Darius was old enough he became obsessed with finding his father. Strange though it sounds, the boy seemed to think that if he could only meet the man, that things could be made right, that they could be a real father and son. But he never did find him. Before Darius was killed he had some kind of premonition of what was about to happen. He brought me this medallion . . . and talked like somehow I was supposed to have it." He paused thoughtfully. "I wonder if he had a premonition of more than his death. I wonder if he somehow could foresee all of this. . . ."

Jared said, "What are you trying to get at?"

Tellico looked him in the eye. "Darius Cottler never found his father. But we have."

Tellico picked up the leatherbound portrait from the bedside table.

"I went out to the Davison cabin alone, just looking around, and found signs somebody had been there shortly before. And I found this in the snow." He opened the case and showed the portrait to Jared.

"The woman bears a strong resemblance to Darius Cottler. I didn't notice that at first—but then I discovered this."

He held up the medallion and the portrait, and slid the medallion into a depression on the leatherbound case. It fit perfectly.

"Darius said the medallion was a token of his father, the only thing he had that had been his. And the medallion obviously came from this case. The killer wasn't Frank Coop. It was—is—Darius Cottler's father."

Jared pondered it, then rejected it. "That's insane, Tellico. I can't believe that."

"Remember what Martha Davison said when we talked to her—how little Geoffrey saw a face in his window before the first murders? Go ask Geoffrey if the face was young or old. Ask him if it was red-haired or gray. Go talk to Claude Gregory when he's able—ask him if it was a red-haired man who broke into his place and nearly killed him."

Jared took the medallion from Tellico. He fingered it. "All right," he said. "I'll ask. But if you're right . . ."

"The danger isn't over," Tellico completed for him.

"I hope to heaven you're wrong."

"I'm not."

Lee Weller, his head bowed, closed the door to Isaiah's bedroom and shuffled over to the bedside. There he stood wordless.

"Lee, what can I do for you?" Isaiah asked.

"I want to give you something," Lee said. Never raising his head, he handed his mail-order catalog to the preacher.

"What's this?"

"It has pictures in it. Of ladies," Lee mumbled. "I . . . look at them."

"Oh." Isaiah laid the catalog on his lap. "Why did you bring it to me?"

"Because it was all my fault, all the people getting killed. God made it happen because I looked so much at the pictures."

"Why do you think that?"

Lee seemed surprised at the question. "Because of you, Preacher Cable. The things you say in the church."

Isaiah was amazed. "But how have I made you think that God would actually cause murders because of such a little thing as you looking at this?"

"But you said there's no little sins, Preacher Cable. You said that, and that God punishes sin unless we confess it."

Isaiah thoughtfully repeated, "Unless we confess it."

"I never confessed about the pictures, Preacher Cable," the childlike Lee said. "I just kept on and kept on doing it." His lip trembled and tears came. "But I didn't think nobody would die because of it. I just didn't want to have to tell, that's all."

Isaiah looked at him with moistening eyes. "It wasn't your fault, Lee."

Lee mulled that over. "Really, Preacher Cable?"

"Really. Let that burden be gone from you. I know how heavy it can be." He hesitated as if unsure whether to say more, but then he continued. "For a while I thought the killing was my fault, Lee. I really did. You see, there are more men in this town than you with unconfessed sins."

But Lee wasn't listening now; he felt purged. "Thank you, Preacher Cable. I don't want to do wrong things, not really. But sometimes I do."

"The apostle Paul had the same difficulty, Lee. You are in good company."

When Lee was gone the old preacher thought about what had just transpired. Eventually he went to sleep, but after only a few minutes a hand touched him. He looked up.

"Hello, Isaiah," Doc Hull said. "I need to talk to you."

Isaiah wiped the sleep from his eyes.

"What is it, Logan?"

"This town thinks the killer is dead. He's not."

Isaiah was confused. "But Rupert said . . ."

"A man named Frank Coop died. But he wasn't the killer. Isaiah, the thing we were afraid of, the thing you and me and Claude have all been worrying about—it's true."

Isaiah grew pale. "How can you possibly think that?"

"I talked to Claude not an hour ago. It was no red-haired man who attacked Matty and him. It was . . . him. Claude recognized him."

Isaiah closed his eyes. "Does anybody else know?"

"I saw Jared going in to talk to Claude himself only a little while ago."

Tears brimmed in the preacher's eyes. "Why can't what's dead and gone stay that way?"

"Because it never was dead and gone at all. We only thought it was. We thought we could be silent and it would never find us out. It's almost funny, really. We seemed to think sin was restricted to the Ruperts and Ingersolls. But not us, not the holy men with the Bibles in our hands. And all the while it was eating us up inside, gnawing like vermin."

"I don't want to hear it."

"That's our problem, Isaiah—we never wanted to hear it. But now we have to hear it. And tell it."

"I couldn't bear that."

"We have no choice. People are dead because of something we did."

Isaiah suddenly became defiant. "No. I don't believe it. I won't. The killer is dead, just as dead as that man we buried years ago."

"Claude recognized him, Isaiah."

"Claude's a fool."

Doc pondered his friend, then rose. "You're lying to yourself, Isaiah."

Rage surged within the preacher. "Damn you, Logan!" he shouted. "Damn your filthy soul!"

"That's right—it is filthy. As black as yours from carrying a secret for too many years."

As Doc left the room, Isaiah grasped at the nearest thing at hand and threw it after him. It was Lee's catalog, and it slammed against the wall and fell to the floor, opening to reveal plump etched women in etched undergarments.

Jared, fresh from a disturbing meeting with Claude Gregory, sat on a snowy step with his elbow on his knee and his forehead resting on the heel of his hand. Tellico had been right. It was no red-haired man who had attacked Claude and Matty. It had been an old man with a long gray beard. Claude had confessed it with surprising reluctance.

"Why didn't you say something, Claude!" Jared had exploded. "You've sat up here and let this town believe it is safe when all the time the real killer is still out there, alive!"

Claude had not answered. He just sat and rubbed

the place where his thumb had been, while Matty ordered Jared out.

Now Jared faced the prospect of telling the town the thing it would least expect and least want.

Somebody approached. It was Doc Hull.

"Come to the church, Jared," Doc said. "I have a story to tell you. It will answer your questions."

Jared nodded, rose, and followed Doc to the church as fine new flakes of snow spat from the sky. He dreaded what he was about to hear, but knew he had to hear it.

In the church house Doc took a deep breath, closed his eyes for a moment, and began his story.

Chapter 18

The Western North Carolina Mountains, Autumn 1845

The storm came over the mountain like a rampaging beast, and the forest cowered before it, bending and trembling. The maples gave up the last of their leaves, leaving only the hardier beeches and oaks to cling to the twisted hulls of their dead summer foliage.

Through a massive thicket of laurel, five men ran from the coming rain. They laughed when the rain poured upon them long before they were near shelter.

In the lead ran Jubal Wallen, the most fleet despite his stocky build. He darted between the laurel tangles with his rifle muzzle-forward as if he were in a bayonet charge. At the top of the rise overlooking the hollow where the cabin stood he stopped and turned to the others coming up behind.

"Isaiah Cable, you're slower than your dullest sermon!" he shouted down at the lean, black-haired man who scrambled up toward him, grinning in the driving rain. "Not yet forty and you run like an old man!"

Isaiah came to Jubal's side, panting, and slapped Jubal's shoulder. "And you chatter like an old woman," he said.

Jubal laughed again, his ruddy face bright even

on this murky afternoon. That was one of the things Isaiah loved about this man—brightness seemed to pour out of him, sparkling in his eyes and enriching his laughter.

Logan Hull reached them, followed a second later by Claude Gregory, whose soggy, shuck-colored hair hung around his face like an inverted bowl. The fifth man, Jubal's brother, Turner, owner of the cabin and long-time resident of these Carolina mountains, came up last. The others were his guests and he didn't think it proper to run ahead of them.

"Let's head in, gentlemen," he said. "We'll cook up some of Jubal's venison."

Jubal had drawn first blood on this hunting expedition three days before with a single well-placed shot, and he had not tired of bragging about it. They had been here four days now, greenhorn hunters following Turner along the winding valleys and the limestone slopes, killing a little game and scaring off a lot that Turner by himself would have easily brought down. But Turner hadn't become impatient. This was the first time he had seen his younger brother Jubal in six years, and he was happy.

They dried out beside the fire, listening to the venison sizzle in the pan. Then they ate like starved men and drank a gallon of coffee. Outside thunder rolled across the sky like a mythological god. When night came the cabin was a warm pocket of golden light on the dark expanse of the mountains.

When conversation had waned and the men were sated and content, Turner suddenly lifted his head as if listening. A moment later someone rapped on the door.

The man whom Turner let in was as rain soaked and rumpled as a stray dog, and smelling almost like one. He was a humped-over caricature of a man, with thick brows and a short, wide nose. He turned his intense eyes around the room, looking at the strangers with concern.

"Who this, Turner, who this?" he demanded in a squeaking voice.

"Relax, Doyle," Turner said. "This is my brother and some of his friends. You've heard me talk about Jubal."

"Jubal? Oh yeah. Jubal."

"Gentlemen, meet Doyle Honaker. Old friend of mine."

Nods were exchanged, then Doyle said, "Got some meat left, Turner?"

The man was even more fascinating when he ate. He put on a loud-slurping, greasy exhibition as he downed a fat-marbled slice of meat, seemingly without chewing, pulling the food down his throat like a snake eating a mouse. None but Turner had seen anything like it. It was all Jubal could do to keep from laughing.

When Doyle's meal was through, Turner asked, "What brings you down tonight?"

"I think our old hermit has kilt somebody," he said.

Isaiah firmly shook his head. "No man is pure evil," he said. "However bad this hermit might be, there's some trace of holiness buried within him."

Turner said, "You don't know this fellow like we do."

"You some kind of preacher or something?" Doyle Honaker asked.

"I am. I pastor a congregation in Indiana," Isaiah responded.

"You a good preacher?"

"I like to think so."

"Ain't narry such a thing. That's like dry water or an honest lawyer." Doyle dropped open his mouth and wheezed. It took Isaiah a moment to realize it was a laugh.

Isaiah smiled politely. "I'll accept the joke. But I still maintain this man cannot be as thoroughly perverse as you say. What's his name, anyway?"

"He's never told and nobody's never asked. He's a devil as far as I'm concerned," Doyle said.

Turner walked to the fireplace and knocked the ashes from his pipe. "Preacher, Doyle's not exaggerating. There's something bad wrong with that man. I run upon him once, and you know what he was doing? Pulling some fresh-hatched mockingbirds out of a nest and mashing them under his boot—a slow crush. Like to have made me sick. The man's sin on two legs, in my book."

"Do you really think he's killed someone?" Jubal asked.

At that, Turner lit his pipe and looked wryly at Doyle. "Don't take this wrong, Doyle, but it wasn't two weeks ago you swore you saw a two-headed bear." One of the others snickered; Doyle looked offended.

"I'm telling you, there's a dead man up there!" Doyle said. "Probably somebody gone looking for the old hermit's silver."

"Silver?" two of them said at once.

Turner blew a smoke ring. "There's a legend hereabouts about an old Indian silver mine somewhere in the mountains. I never gave it much credence, but a lot of folks believe the hermit knows where it is and has a lot of silver stashed away."

"Could it be true?"

"Could be, I suppose. There has been some silver found here and there."

"What are we going to do about the dead man?" Doyle said.

"Go up and check tomorrow, I reckon," Turner said.

* * *

When morning came, the rain had dwindled to a sluggish drizzle. Across the Carolina ridges fog rose from land to sky, drifting between the mountains like smoke. Turner, his four guests, and Doyle rode across the sodden land toward the mountain where the hermit lived —a man who in the minds of the four newcomers had become monstrous.

"Does he always live alone?" Isaiah asked.

"Not entirely. Off and on there's a young fellow with him a lot, a raggedy-looking devil they say is his son. He's full-grown and mean as the old man."

"Think the younger one will be there?" Jubal asked.

"I ain't seen him in a spell," Doyle said. "But you can't never tell—he comes and goes."

"Where'd the old fellow come from?"

"Nobody knows."

"How does he live? Does he ever spend any of that silver he's supposed to have?"

"Not to my knowledge," Turner said. "He hunts, fishes. That's about it."

The wind grew colder as they rode, and when they entered a narrow valley lined with mossy rocks, Isaiah felt a mood of oppression come upon him. This was a dark and somber place.

He wanted to turn back. But he said nothing of it out of pride. He glanced about at his companions. From their looks he suspected they felt similarly uneasy.

"Where'd you see the body, Doyle?" Turner asked. They had been riding silently for several minutes now, and Isaiah started as Turner's words unexpectedly broke the quiet.

"Up yonder beside the shack," Doyle said. "Sprawled out right in the open."

They dismounted as a group and tied the horses.

"Tie 'em loose in case we have to get back on fast," Turner advised, which did nothing to ease the fears of the others.

Turner parted some brambles with his hand to give them a view. Atop a hill they saw a dark and almost shapeless shack on a pine-covered hilltop. They watched it a long time. Nothing moved. There was no evidence of life about it.

"Maybe the old man really is dead," Doyle said.

"Let's go see," Turner said.

"Should we take our rifles?" Jubal asked.

"No. Me and Doyle will take our pistols. If he's still alive and sees strangers coming up armed it might spook him."

Turner took the lead, Doyle right behind him and the others trailing.

"Phew!" Claude said. "Something's dead, that's for sure!"

"Doyle, you were right," Turner said. He pointed. A body lay crumpled in the leaves beside the shack's door.

Wrinkling their noses against the smell, and dreading to see the body up close because they knew the birds would already have worked on it, the four future elders of the Jerusalem Camp church approached behind the two leaders. Turner stopped short.

"That ain't the hermit," he said. His voice dropped almost to a whisper. "That's just a boy."

Isaiah looked closely and saw he was right. A boy in his mid-teens. He was dead. There was a rifle-ball hole in his forehead.

"Is this his son?" Isaiah asked.

"No," Turner responded. "Looks familiar, but I can't place him."

The men gathered around the corpse. Claude

turned away, making the sounds of barely stifled regurgitation.

"Why would he kill a boy?" Turner said. Suddenly he gave in to a burst of indignation. He drew the pistol he always carried and stomped over to the shack. He kicked open the door and went inside. A moment later he was out again. He holstered the pistol.

"Nobody here. Murdering old sod is gone."

"What are you doing at my place?" a voice from nearby said.

The group wheeled about as one. An incredibly dirty, bedraggled man with long hair and a longer beard stood beside a pine on a small rise to the east. He carried a rifle, but it was not leveled.

"This is my place. Get away."

Turner said, "The hell we will. Did you do this?" He gestured at the dead body.

The man shifted the rifle just a little. Turner's hand moved toward his pistol. Isaiah wished he had brought his rifle. "That was an accident," the man said.

"Sure it was. Why did you do it?"

"I didn't. The boy was out hunting with some others. One of 'em shot him and run off. My son's gone to tell this boy's folks what happened."

"You're a liar," Doyle cut in. "This boy's been dead at least two days. What did he do—wander too close to your silver?"

The man on the rise made a strange gesture with his lips and shook his head. Then a lot of things happened very fast.

He lifted his muzzle-loader and shot Doyle through the heart. Turner shouted and drew his pistol, but the hermit drew a flintlock from his belt and shot him, too.

The others scattered, diving for cover, but Jubal

made a guttural noise and ran to his fallen brother. He knelt, cried out, then picked up his brother's dropped pistol and shot the man on the hill. The ball hit him in the lower body. He grimaced, put his hands on his belly as if suffering a stomachache, and crumpled over.

Doyle was dead, but Turner wasn't. The bullet had torn a shallow path through his side without puncturing anything vital, and though the impact had stunned him, he came around quickly and did not seem in particularly bad shape.

Jubal sat against a tree, crying.

"What are we going to do?" Logan Hull asked.

"This is terrible," Isaiah said. "Terrible . . . I'm a minister of the gospel. I can't be associated with something like—"

"Shut up, both of you! Let me think," Turner said. At the same time, thunder pealed and the wind kicked up. It was a moist wind, riding the head of a new storm. A few moments later the first drops fell.

"Into the shack," Turner directed. "Somebody needs to patch me up a bit, anyway."

Isaiah glanced at Claude. Both men were shaking. Claude came near Isaiah. "I feel sick," he whispered.

"I can't be associated with this," Isaiah repeated. "It would ruin me. Ruin me."

They walked to the cabin. "Somebody bring in Doyle," Turner said. "Ain't right to let him get rained on."

Isaiah and Claude both swallowed with dry throats and turned to Doyle's body. The dead face was now very white. They did not want to touch him, but did.

When they came in from the rain, dragging Doyle's body in, they found Turner holding a candle and staring at handfuls of silver molded into crude oval slugs that looked almost like coins.

"So, it's true after all," Turner said very softly. "Look at it!"

"There must be hundreds, maybe thousands of dollars here," Claude said in a tone of awe. He picked up a double handful and let it clatter back to the tabletop.

For a long time the men were silent.

"What should we do with this?" Claude asked.

"The silver isn't ours," Logan Hull said.

"No? Then whose?" Claude suddenly had a greedy look. "The man shot at us. I say we got a right to keep it."

"The man has a son."

Turner nodded. "So he does. But he ain't here now, is he!"

Logan shook his head. "It isn't right. We owe it to the folks of whoever that dead boy is to tell what happened." He said the words, but they didn't matter now and he knew it. A decision had already been made among them, unspoken but fully known.

"You realize, Claude, that I can't be associated with this," Isaiah said. He was still shaking.

Lightning crackled in the west. Branches grappled skyward in the wind like the hands of old men. Jubal began patching Turner's wound.

It took a long time for the rain to stop, and a very long time to dig the hole, so when they were done it was nearly sunset. The mud-covered men dragged the bodies of the murdered boy and the hermit to the hole's edge. The rain began falling again, but this time it was gentle.

"I suppose we ought to say a prayer?" said Isaiah.

The suggestion fell among the men like deadweight; the idea of prayer in these circumstances was a travesty.

"Which one first?" asked Claude.

"Just dump them," Turner spat.

The boy's stiff body made a gruesome slapping sound against the mud at the bottom of the hole. It landed facedown. Brown water pooled around it. The back of the head was terrible where the ball had exited.

"I can't believe we're doing this," Logan murmured.

"Shut up," Claude said. "You're as much a part of it as the rest of us."

"You want the silver, that's all," Logan said, but Claude pretended not to hear.

They dragged the hermit's body over and threw it in, too. "We should have made the hole deeper," Jubal said.

Suddenly they sensed another presence; the awareness flew among them like a whispered message. Turning, they saw a slender young man standing near the spot where the hermit had fallen. He was mud-covered and wet, had olive-toned skin and jet-black hair. His beard was thin and straight.

"What did you do to my father?" the newcomer said.

"He had an accident," Turner responded, walking toward the fellow. "He cut himself and bled to death."

"You're lying." The young man backed away. He had no visible weapons.

"Come and take a look yourself," Turner said.

"No."

"Come on. You can trust me."

"No."

Turner drew his pistol and shot the youth through the head. Isaiah screamed. His cry echoed across the drenched mountains like the shot that preceded it.

They dumped the boy atop his father. Now even

Logan knew there could be no turning back—this was clear-cut murder.

Claude took the shovel and began madly tossing muddy dirt atop the still forms. He packed it crudely around them with the blade of the shovel.

Jubal blanched. "God, Claude, slow down—you've sliced off the last one's thumb," he said.

Claude did not slow down.

When the burying was done they spread leaves over the grave to hide it. They took the silver from the shack, Doyle's body they put atop the table, and set the shack on fire. They took the silver back to Turner's cabin, silently.

Chapter 19

"Things were different from then on," Doc Hull said. "We never knew if anybody ever came asking about any of the dead ones. We kept part of the silver, and Turner Wallen kept some. But we never had the heart to spend much of it. Blood money, you know.

"We went back to Indiana, never telling a soul what had happened. But we could hardly look each other in the eye. When the Mexican War started, I volunteered. So did Claude. Isaiah kept on preaching, and Jubal just kept hoarding the silver. Too guilt-ridden and afraid to spend it, yet unwilling to let it go. It destroyed him before it was through."

Jared had been listening with his forehead resting in his hands, his elbows on his knees. Now he looked up. "Are you saying the rumors were true—Jubal killed himself?"

Doc nodded. "I passed it off as caused by his heart. We folded his hands in the coffin to cover the slash on his wrist. Another deception we 'elders' agreed to. It was guilt that made him do it, and fear."

"Fear of what?"

Doc's answer raised bumps on Jared's arms. "Of the hermit. He dreamed of him. Funny, it doesn't seem so ridiculous now."

"What finally happened to the silver?"

Doc smiled sadly. "We used some of it to establish this town. God forgive us, we used part of that money to build this very church house."

Jared's heart was pounding hard. "I never would have dreamed Pa could do such a thing."

"Your pa's a good man. But a man he is, not a god."

Jared stood and paced. He craned back his neck, trying to ease the mounting tension in his muscles. "But if the hermit is dead, how can what's happening here relate to him?"

"We thought he was dead. Maybe he wasn't. He might have dug his way out of that grave—it was shallow enough, and the dirt was loose and muddy." Doc looked at the floor. "It must have been like digging out of hell."

"And all these years he's been looking and planning, trailing all of you. . . ."

"Apparently so."

"What about the son? It might be him."

Doc shook his head. "There was no question he was dead. I examined him too closely to doubt it. His father I did not."

Jared asked, "You say you used part of the silver to begin the town. What happened to the rest?"

"When Jubal killed himself, your father and Claude and I decided to get rid of it. They gave it to me and told me to hide it where it would never be found. I'm the only one who knows today where it is."

Jared was silent a long time. "My own father. Preaching and leading a church. And all these years hiding a killing and a theft."

"Don't reject your father, Jared. He needs you."

Doc looked at him, his face sad. Jared went to the door, pausing to ask, "Whatever happened to Turner Wallen?"

"He vanished shortly after it all happened."

Jared felt a chill. "So he was the first."

"Yes."

"And now, thirty-five years later, it happens again. And all of Jerusalem Camp pays the price for the sin of its elders." Jared spoke thoughtfully. "The sins of the fathers are visited upon the sons."

He slammed the door as he left. Doc closed his eyes and took a deep breath.

Isaiah stirred on his bed, rolled over, and slowly awakened. Jared sat beside him, staring coldly, and immediately Isaiah knew the secret had been told.

"Logan told you?" he asked.

Jared nodded.

"I never wanted you to know."

"I don't understand, Pa. Hiding dead men, taking their silver, never telling even of the dead boy you found. Do you think his family ever knew what happened to him? They may still be out there somewhere, wondering."

"Don't, Jared. Don't you think I've gone through all that in my mind every day of my life? There's been hardly a night I haven't dreamed of that open grave, the dead bodies. . . ."

"But one of them not really dead after all."

Isaiah shuddered. "Yes."

"It's your fault, Pa, you and the other elders. The Davisons, Red, Sean, Horace . . . paid for what you did. You've stood in that pulpit for thirty-five years since then, telling others to confess and repent of their sins and accept forgiveness. And you and Doc and Claude sitting there covering and nursing your own guilt . . . in a church house paid for with stolen silver."

Isaiah turned his back on Jared. His shoulders heaved. A sudden burst of sorrow rose in Jared, but dissolved like smoke. A gulf too wide to cross lay between his father and himself.

There was a noise. Doc Hull stood in the doorway. Doc came to Jared and put his hand on his shoulder. Jared shrugged it off like it was foul.

"Leave Isaiah alone for now, Jared," Doc said. "He isn't in condition for this kind of confrontation. It could kill him."

Inwardly, Jared wanted to put his arms around his father, but felt frozen in his place.

"I've got to go," Jared said. "I've got to tell a town who thinks it is out of danger that it really isn't. And convince it that Frank Coop wasn't their killer after all. Don't worry . . . I won't tell your secret. I don't have the stomach to admit that my own father . . ." He faltered and stopped.

Jared rose and walked out the door, slamming it behind him. Anna waited in the front room, an inquisitive and slightly frightened expression on her face. Jared stalked past her, put on his coat and snowshoes in silence, and left.

In the bedroom Doc remained with Isaiah, who now had stopped crying and was staring at the ceiling.

"I've lost my son because of you," Isaiah said.

"Somebody else lost a son thirty-five years ago and we just hid it away," Doc responded.

"Get out of here, Logan."

Looking older and more stooped than ever, Doc Hull shuffled out of the room.

Jared looked across a crowd of expressionless faces. He sensed their disbelief even before it was voiced.

Bolivar Brooks, brother of the late Louis, stood with his hat in his hands. "Jared, I don't buy it. Frank Coop had to be the killer. Otherwise, we have to believe there were two murderers in one isolated mountain town in one winter. That's too much to swallow." Among the crowd Jared heard murmurs of agreement.

Bolivar continued, "Jerusalem Camp has lived peacefully for years until suddenly this Tellico shows up, refusing to tell who he is, pretending to be some kind of town guardian, and acting as if he were a help to you, Jared. I think maybe he fooled you, fooled us all. It's clear Coop came after Tellico. Tellico brought this . . . killing winter to Jerusalem Camp. Seems to me he's likely to be wanted by the law somewhere, with associations like he's got."

Jared said, "Frank Coop came after Tellico for personal reasons. It was strictly between the two of them. He had no motive to have done any of the murders."

"What about Clyde Ingersoll?" Once again the crowd murmured, more animated now.

"He saw Ingersoll moving on the other side of a window and probably thought it was Tellico."

Someone in the group said, "You're going to have to do better than that, Jared. If Coop wasn't the killer, who was?"

Jared faltered. He lacked the will to reveal his father's secret, and had pledged not to do so besides. He looked across the crowd, bewildered, feeling almost as guilty as the elders themselves, for now he was hiding the secret just like they.

Suddenly he noticed Claude Gregory at the rear. Jared's eye caught Claude's; Claude broke the gaze at once.

"Claude, tell them," Jared said. "Was the man who attacked you Frank Coop?"

Claude's eyes darted as every man turned to him. He looked like a trapped rabbit. "Well . . ." Jared saw the struggle going on within the man. "Yes. It was Coop."

Jared's legs almost went out from under him. "That's not what you said when . . ." He stopped. It was useless. The battle was lost.

Bolivar said, "Jared, I'm sorry. I think you're telling what you think is the truth, but the strain has got to you. You need to relax for a while and forget what we've been through. All we need to do now is keep Tellico under guard and wait for spring. It's over now, Jared, and you've got to let it go."

"I'll let it go all right," Jared said. He reached beneath his vest and removed the homemade tin star the town council had given him. He plopped it on the pulpit in front of him. "I'm officially through as marshal of Jerusalem Camp. If you're not going to believe you're still in danger, then I've got no choice but to protect my family and leave the rest of you to yourselves. I can't guard all of you alone, and the one man who would be willing to help me you're treating like a prisoner.

"The real killer is still out there. He's an old man with an old grudge against some in this town." He met Claude's eye; the old man immediately looked away. "He'll be back. He's got a long-standing debt to pay off."

"Who's he got a grudge against?" Bolivar asked skeptically.

"Ask Claude," Jared said, descending the platform and walking down the center aisle to the church door. He turned before he left and said, "Be careful. I'm warning you. It isn't over yet."

When he was gone, Bolivar turned to Claude, whose face looked white as the snow outside. "What's he talking about, Claude?"

"I don't know. It was Frank Coop who attacked me. I swear it was. I swear."

* * *

In the night Isaiah lay in silence, still thinking about what had happened earlier in the evening.

Jared had returned from his town meeting at the church house and described what had happened there. Then he had put his arms around Isaiah and told him he loved him. And forgave him.

Isaiah cried the most purging cry of his life. It was as if an ancient wall of ice inside him started to melt. For the first time in thirty-five years, atoning for his silence began to seem more important than keeping his secret.

"It's up to me," he whispered to the ceiling. He rose and stood, a pale figure in a pale nightshirt.

He dressed as quietly as he could, putting on his old black coat and hat and Jared's snowshoes. He left the house with his Bible in hand.

The night was cold. Trudging down the hill, finding walking difficult because of his apoplexy and his long idleness, he nevertheless felt better than he had in months. His beloved church house loomed invitingly below. There he could think and pray and read his Bible, and God would send him the answer he needed. He would show him how to make it right.

Quietly he quoted, "Have mercy upon me, O God, according to thy lovingkindness: according unto the multitude of thy tender mercies blot out my transgressions. . . ."

Panting for breath, he continued toward the church.

Chapter 20

Lee Weller bolted awake with a cry. He had just dreamed of a face at his window. He sat up in his bunk and scrambled for a match, with which he lit the kerosene lamp on the upturned crate beside his bed. He pulled his knees to his chest and wrapped his arms around them.

Only a dream. But when he looked at his window he cried out again, for the face really was there.

An old man, with long gray hair and a heavy beard. The eyes were amazingly intense.

Lee leaped from his bed, knocking over the kerosene lamp as he did so. Burning oil poured across the floor.

He turned the lamp upright, pulled a blanket from his bunk, and beat out the pool of flames. When that was done he looked at the window again. The old man was gone.

His heart racing, Lee squatted to the floor, shaking.

That was the same man he had seen at the edge of the forest several days ago. The one he had tried to pretend was imaginary—at least since everybody had been talking about the killer being dead and the danger over.

But what if they were wrong like Jared said they were?

But I'm not smart, Lee reminded himself. Everybody says I don't think good, don't know much about nothing.

He sat on the floor beside the flickering lamp, afraid to move, wondering what he should do.

Shortly thereafter, Bolivar Brooks arose from his own bed in his house across town. Alone there—for his wife always wintered in San Francisco and had been gone since before the first snow—he had heard movement in his kitchen.

Clad only in long underwear, he carried his Remington gingerly, tiptoeing down the narrow hallway.

At the door to the kitchen he stopped, took a deep breath, then quickly stepped inside, saying, "Hold it right there!"

In the darkness he saw nothing. Then he made out a still form at the table. "Who are you?" he said, thumbing back the pistol's hammer. But the figure did not move.

He edged forward—still it sat motionless—and from a shelf Bolivar pulled a match. He struck it on the kitchen hearth and raised it as it flared.

What he had seen at the table was not a man. It was a big fur cloak, heaped between the edge of the table and the back of a chair so it looked in the dark like a human figure. Confused, Bolivar stared at the cloak until the match burned his fingers and he dropped it.

The room went dark and something darker moved in the corner behind him. He did not see it. It fell upon him and after that he saw nothing at all.

The Gray Man put on his cloak. He left the house and looked down the dark street. From behind the closed shutters of the church house a light shone. He quietly moved toward it.

* * *

Tellico helplessly examined the small window in the room, knowing he could never squeeze through it. Two guards remained in the main room, and the odds of convincing them that he had seen something important would be as likely as convincing them just to let him walk out.

But he had to get out, for he had seen Isaiah walking down toward the church—and later another figure had moved across the snow far below. A man, creeping around the church from the other side.

What could he do? Tellico's two guards were more than he could hope to overcome by himself. One of them was built like a bull and the other was edgy enough to be dangerous.

From the talk of the guards Tellico had gathered something of what had happened; the townsfolk had refused to believe Frank Coop wasn't the one responsible for all the killings, and Jared had resigned in disgust.

The light in Jared's house was out. Right now Jared probably was asleep inside; he must be, or else he would have detected his father leaving the house.

How to warn him? Tellico's mind probed his options. At last he went to the door of his room and listened. He heard rumbling snores; at least one guard was sleeping. He tried the door, but it was locked.

"Hey, friend!" he said through the door, careful not to speak too loudly. "Friend!"

He heard somebody approach the door, but—as he had hoped—the snoring continued in the background. Only one guard was awake.

"What do you want?" said a sleepy voice just beyond the door.

"I'm dying of thirst in here," Tellico said. "Bring me a drink of water."

Muttering, the man moved away. The snores continued.

Tellico steeled himself, waiting, and breathed a prayer.

Jared awakened at the first knock. He went to the door with his shotgun leveled before him.

"Tellico, how did you get . . ."

"No time, Jared. Listen, I saw your father leave the house; I think he went to the church. But I saw someone else moving down there, too."

The possible implications of that took a moment to register in Jared's drowsy mind. "Oh no," he said. He ran back to Isaiah's room—indeed it was empty—then into his own room, where he tossed off a brief, confusing explanation to his wife as he threw on his clothes. He checked his shotgun.

"Can't find my snowshoes. Pa must have taken them," he said to Tellico. He stepped out into the snow.

"How'd you get loose?" he asked as he waded through the thick accumulation.

"One was asleep. The other I knocked out and caught before he hit the floor. It wasn't easy."

They trekked quickly down toward the church.

The Gray Man smiled at Isaiah across the tip of his upraised long knife. Isaiah's face was a white mask, its expression of fear accented by his drooping, stroke-afflicted mouth.

"So, it is you," Isaiah said.

"Indeed," the Gray Man said. "Back from the grave of corpses, where a man hugs the dead body of his son and fights for breath. Have you ever breathed death, Preacher?" He spat out the final word like a mouthful of bad water. "Can you imagine what it is to dig yourself out of the earth itself and find your home just a smoldering ruin and all your wealth taken? That is what you did to me, you and your companions."

Isaiah withdrew until his back was against the pulpit. "It was never our intention to hurt you—we didn't go there to wrong you."

"But wrong me you did, Isaiah Cable. Yes, I know your name. I know all about you, and about Claude Gregory and Logan Hull. Even the dead Jubal Wallen. I've made Claude pay already. Now your turn. Logan Hull will be last."

He thinks Claude died in the fire, Isaiah thought. For Claude's sake that was one misconception he would not correct. "How did you learn our names?" Isaiah asked.

"Turner Wallen was a talkative man with the right persuasion," the Gray Man said. "He died talking, talking. I would have found you more quickly if the war hadn't taken you away. I lost your trail for many, many years, but I never forgot you. Now my time is drawing near. I will not go to my grave without sending you, my old attackers—and as many of your people as I can—to their own. That I vow before heaven and before hell."

"I am a man of God. You mustn't harm me."

"Man of God?" The Gray Man shook his head. "I know you for what you are, Preacher. You are a child of Satan, just like me."

He advanced, still speaking. "It has taken me more than three decades to find you, but my life has been well occupied. I'm a bloodthirsty old devil, I am. Old and young, male and female . . . I've drained life from them all." He laughed. "Had you succeeded in killing me those years ago you would have saved many lives, Preacher."

Isaiah asked, "The boy we found dead outside your cabin—why did you kill him?"

The Gray Man's smile broadened. "There are pleasures some of us know that your tender preacher's ears would not care to hear about."

Isaiah felt a wave of disgust. "Turner Wallen was right. You are pure evil—and a madman."

"Without a doubt."

The door burst open, and the Gray Man wheeled.

"You leave my friend alone, Mister," Lee Weller said. "You get away from him."

Isaiah slid to his rump on the floor. "Lee, get away. He'll hurt you."

The Gray Man cocked his head, perceiving Lee's slowness of mind. He smiled. "Come to me, my friend. Let me show you my knife. Have you seen one like it?"

"You're bad. You hurt people. Get away from Preacher Cable."

"I don't hurt people, Lee. They hurt themselves. They do things to me that are wrong, and I make them pay."

"Get out, Lee!" Isaiah ordered.

The Gray Man clamped his teeth together and turned on Isaiah. He lunged at him, and the blade struck the preacher in the arm. Isaiah cried out.

Lee bellowed and leaped forward, closing his hands on the Gray Man's throat from behind. The old man almost fell beneath Lee's weight, but balanced himself and lunged upward with the knife. The blade sliced Lee's hand, but Lee wouldn't let go.

Under other circumstances there might have been something comical in the wild dance that went on for nearly a minute—the Gray Man lunging behind him with his knife, vainly trying to reach the determined man who clung to him like a fighting dog.

Suddenly two more were in the room—Jared and Tellico. Jared raised his shotgun and shouted something, but when Isaiah looked back again at Lee and the Gray

Man, Lee had been knocked loose but immediately had been taken hostage, the long knife impressing the skin of his throat.

It was a standoff posed in silence: the preacher, collapsed helplessly at the foot of his pulpit; Lee endangered, his face full of fear; and Jared and Tellico in the open church door, unable to do anything.

"Move aside," the Gray Man said. "I'm leaving here—and if anyone follows me from the town, you'll find this man's head ten feet from his body." As if to make his point, he let the blade tip break Lee's skin; Lee yelped as a few drops of blood ran down the long knife.

Jared and Tellico stepped aside, and the Gray Man exited, taking Lee with him.

Chapter 21

The two men who had guarded Tellico came around the side of the church. The smaller one had a blood-crusted lip.

"Jared, Tellico got away. He hollered for me and . . ." He stopped, having seen Tellico there with Jared. "Hey, what are you—"

"Save it," Jared interrupted. "No time for that. The killer's been back, and Lee Weller's been taken hostage."

"Who's been back?"

"The killer, blast it!"

"But I thought Frank Coop—"

"You thought wrong."

The two newcomers exchanged confused glances. The bigger one, a veteran placer miner named Carlen Flatt, growled out, "You're dreaming, Jared."

"He's telling the truth." The voice was Isaiah's. He stood in the church door, and leaned against the frame. "The man almost killed me. Lee saved my life and was taken hostage for his trouble."

"We've got to go after him," Tellico said. "Should I ring the church bell?"

"No," Jared said. "Our friend in the mountains would hear it and might get spooked—and I don't like to think what he might do to Lee then."

Jared heard a noise and spun, leveling his shotgun. He lowered it again when Witt Essler came into view.

Witt was very white. "Bolivar's dead," he said. "Thumb cut off." He paused long enough to shudder visibly. "I couldn't sleep. . . . I saw somebody leaving Bolivar's place, went over and checked. Bolivar was in the kitchen."

Jared turned to Carlen. "You believe I'm dreaming now?"

Carlen shook his head.

They separated briefly, each preparing himself for the mountains, putting on extra clothing, snowshoes, gathering arms and ammunition. Snow began to fall, quickly growing to a near-blizzard.

"No point in going with the snow like this, Jared," said one of the men when they gathered again, for the group had grown substantially as the town awakened and word spread.

"I'm going, point or not," Jared returned.

"But you're not healed up—"

"I'm going. That's Lee Weller he's got."

Nobody else argued. The wind rose so that the snow seemed not to be falling so much as blowing from west to east. The group set out.

They had barely reached the base of the mountain when it became evident that Tellico could not keep up. He remained somewhat weak from his recent sickness, and his gunshot shoulder ached in the cold. Jared turned to him. In the wind he had to shout. "Turn back, Tellico! We can't slow up for you."

Tellico argued, but Jared prevailed. Tellico turned back, disappointed, feeling helpless. In the driving wind he went back to town. The church still was open; he went inside.

Isaiah was there, Doc Hull beside him. Behind Tellico the sky began to change; morning coming on.

"I couldn't keep up," Tellico said. "Jared ran me off."

"Your return was a godsend," Isaiah said.

"What do you mean?"

Doc Hull came to Tellico and gently touched his wounded shoulder.

"Are you well enough to use a shovel?"

"A shovel? If I had to, I suppose."

"You do. We're going digging for silver."

The old man pushed Lee before him like a mule, prodding him with the knife and threatening him with the Henry.

"Get on, half-wit!" the Gray Man ordered, prodding Lee again. The snow was terrible here, blinding and cold against Lee's face. They were ascending a narrow wash between boulders hard as frozen iron. Lee was numb with cold and beginning to feel faint.

"I can't go on," he said. He sank to his knees.

The old man cursed and raised the blade. As it descended Lee dodged it, more out of luck than design. Blindly he punched at his captor; his fist sank deep into the fur cloak and the man grunted and fell.

Lee rose and ran upward, hoping for escape. On up the slope he slid on ice and fell back. He tumbled into the Gray Man and together they rolled like human snowballs several yards. Lee struck his head, and when he stood he had difficulty focusing his eyes. In his blurred vision he saw the Gray Man draw near, blood on his face, the knife up and ready to stab.

Lee lunged desperately to his left, plunging over a bluff and disappearing into the whiteness below.

* * *

Tellico, ignoring as best he could the pain of his shoulder, dug the shovel again and again into the dirt on the grave-pocked hillside overlooking Jerusalem Camp. The ground had been frozen about a foot down into the grave, but now he was in softer moist dirt, and the work was going faster. The cross atop the grave slid slowly to the right and fell, turning the etched name of Jubal Wallen to the snow-spitting clouds.

Tellico wondered why the devil he was doing this. Doc hadn't fully explained. At the moment Doc droned on in a steady monotone to Isaiah, who had no business on the hillside in his condition, but who had refused to go back home to his bed. Most of what he said meant nothing to Tellico.

". . . I knew that here it would never be found, Isaiah. And it seemed fitting, letting Jubal keep it with him—the thing that so obsessed his last years. The silver killed him, and the guilt. Like Judas Iscariot, you know."

The shovel hit wood. Tellico looked at the two old men beside the grave. Their faces were white and pasty.

He dug until the coffin's redwood top was finally uncovered. He paused. "Are you sure you want to do this?"

Isaiah looked uncertain. But Doc firmly nodded.

Tellico broke the lock on the coffin. He stepped out of the grave, caught the lid with the edge of the shovel, and slowly pulled it open.

What was revealed caused all of them to draw in their breath.

Decay had left only a gray skull where Jubal's head had rested. Bony hands lay folded together, leathery skin clinging to the knuckles. But the overall shape remained that of Jubal in life: a hefty man, barrel-chested.

Then it all began to change.

As snow and wind blew across the skull, it began to crack and crumble, seemingly blowing away. Then it collapsed, and a moment later the broad chest crumbled as well, the black frock coat falling flat. But not at the center of the chest cavity, where the coat draped the outline of a small box.

"Logan—you put it inside him!" Isaiah exclaimed.

"It was easy enough," Doc answered. "A quick incision on the slab, the strongbox slipped inside the chest. It struck me as appropriate, somehow."

"Just get it out and cover him back up," Isaiah said, turning away.

Jared lowered his shotgun and called the alert. "It's Lee! Hold your fire!"

Lee it was, stumbling down the hillside. Thirty feet from them he fell and rolled, almost burying himself in snow. Jared was the first at his side. He put a finger on Lee's neck. "Alive—but near froze. We have to get him back to town. Carlen, will you take him?"

"I might be needed up here, Jared."

"You're the only man big enough to carry him," Jared responded. Carlen thought about it a moment, then nodded.

"Good. Don't go slow—he might end up losing some toes if you do." Jared rubbed Lee's face. "Lee—you're all right now. We're getting you home."

Lee's eyelids fluttered. He flashed a weak smile. "Thank you, Mister Jared."

"Where is he?"

"Yonder . . . up the hill. I fell a long way. Into the snow."

"Do you know where he was going?"

"I think to High Ridge, Mister Jared."

"We'll get him, Lee."

With Lee supported on his broad shoulder, Carlen went back down the mountain toward town as the blizzard churned about them.

With Witt at his side, Jared led the group farther up the incline. The effort seemed almost futile, but Jared wasn't going to turn back. It was time for conclusion, for final encounter. No longer was it unwilling marshal facing unknown enemy. It was Jared Cable, going after a flesh-and-blood devil who had threatened his father.

He wished he could have known before now that the killer was making for High Ridge, for he knew a shortcut. But they were too far up this route to take another.

Up they climbed into the great circle of mountains around Jerusalem Camp. The steep escarpments were heavy with snow, piled in sagging heaps that could drop at the touch of the wind or the shifting of loose rocks.

Their difficult path wound around a mountain knob. The man they pursued left a trail that was remarkably clear; he seemed to be floundering along. It should have sounded a warning to Jared; their prey left too obvious a spoor.

When they were high and the air was thin, Witt suddenly stopped. "Jared . . ."

"What's wrong?"

"I'm not sure. I think—"

A tremendous rumble from above rendered him inaudible. Jared looked up in time to see what looked like the mountain itself bending down toward him. He shouted but could not hear himself. He saw men rushing back, others knocked into the air, at least two swallowed in a vast descending curtain of white. Then he himself was under, his breath driven from his lungs.

* * *

Tellico met Carlen and Lee like a man would meet two ghosts; their forms materialized slowly in the storm, and grew more substantial as they approached.

The silver remained in its box, and the box was slung inside a cloth pack strapped to Tellico's back.

"Where is Jared?" Tellico asked.

Carlen, looking back at him suspiciously, pointed in the direction from which he had come.

"Have they caught him yet?"

Carlen shook his head.

"Where are they heading?"

Carlen's glower remained. "I don't know why I should trust you," he said.

"Because I might be able to stop some people from getting killed," Tellico returned.

Carlen chewed his lip, but Lee answered without hesitation. "High Ridge."

"Is there a shorter way?"

Finally relenting, Carlen answered, "There is, but it's mighty dangerous. You walk the cliff line to the west and cut right up to the ridge. It's a fast way if you can survive it."

"How do I get there?"

Carlen seemed impatient but gave quick directions. Tellico thanked him and turned away. Carlen could see Tellico was weary and weak. He'll not make it, Carlen thought. Last we'll see of him.

"Come on, Lee," Carlen said. "Let's go put some coffee in your belly."

"And pie, Mr. Carlen?"

"And pie."

Jared came to, staring at luminescent gray clouds. A bearded face appeared above him.

"I've been through worse than what just happened to you, pilgrim," said the Gray Man. "I've known what it is to have the earth itself on top of me."

He was perched on a boulder. The wind tugged his beard.

Jared tried to talk; it took four tries before he could get his voice out.

"Where are the others?"

"Snow buried a couple. Another couple got swept over the bluff there. The survivors dug out who they could and left. But they never found you. Must have figured you for dead." The Gray Man made a pushing motion with his hand. "It was easy—one shove and the boulder dropped and set off the snowslide."

Jared stood with effort. He tried to lunge at the seated man, but his movements were slow and forced. He fell short and dropped on his face. The Gray Man laughed.

Jared rolled onto his back and slowly sat up again.

"I'm not sure why I pulled you out," the Gray Man said. "I think it was your face. You remind me of a preacher I first saw about thirty-five years ago at a certain burial back in Carolina. I'd make a wager you're his boy. Right?"

"Let me go."

He laughed. "Well, this is just prime! Old preacherman gives me the slip but I wind up with his boy!"

"Don't kill me. I've got a wife and son."

The old man's expression became bitter. He said, "I had a family myself at one time. A wife, a daughter, a son. I held my son's body in my arms in a grave your pa and his psalm-singing friends put me in. Buried alive just like you were just now."

There came a sudden noise behind Jared. He turned. It was Tellico. He had just come up along the treacherous cliff line. Tellico was panting and pale.

"There was a second son, too, Mister Cottler. He died on a battlefield the day after I met him. His name was Darius."

The Gray Man turned his Henry on Tellico. Jared expected him to shoot Tellico at once, but he didn't. "Who are you?" he asked.

"Call me Tellico. I knew Darius."

"I never knew no Darius."

"He was born after you left home. He fought for the Union in the war. Died for it—and you were on his mind the last night of his life, Mister Cottler."

Jared couldn't interpret Cottler's expression. "You're lying," Cottler said.

"No lie. He searched for you, Mister Cottler. Wanted more than anything to know the father he never saw."

Cottler's thick brows nettled. "You're a liar—I'll blast you to damnation right here!"

With amazing calm Tellico said, "You don't have the power to damn anyone but yourself. You don't really want to kill me. Put down the rifle and come with me. Let me tell you about your son. The last night he lived he talked to me, but in his mind I think maybe he was talking to you."

Cottler seemed very agitated. For a moment Jared thought the old man might actually surrender his weapon, for it was clear Tellico's words intrigued him. But suddenly he cursed and fired a shot. It barely missed Tellico, but Tellico hardly flinched. The sound echoed between the ridges. The mountain gave another grumble as if disturbed in its rest.

"I'm going to show you something, Mister Cottler," Tellico said. Slowly he lifted his hand to his neck and pulled out the medallion. He untied the cord and tossed the metal oval to Cottler. The old man stooped and picked it up. His eyes changed as he recognized it. Then Jared tossed over the leatherbound portrait.

"Where did you get . . ."

"From your son. He carried it because it had belonged to you." Tellico paused. "Darius knew you beat his mother, and he had heard all the rumors. But he never gave up on you. He believed you to be a better man than what people said."

Cottler closed his fist around the medallion.

"Something else for you too," Tellico said. He loosened the strongbox of silver, which he had strapped to him, and threw it to the old man's feet, where it fell open. Some of the silver spilled onto the snow.

"They tell me that's yours," Tellico said. "If it is, take it."

Suddenly the mountain rumbled again, then made a cracking noise followed by another rumble.

Tellico extended his hand to Jared, who lay below the narrow ledge on which Tellico stood. "Up!" he ordered. "Get away from there!"

Jared rose. Cottler ignored him. He was looking at the medallion in his hand. Jared reached up; Tellico took his hand and pulled him higher. Grimacing, Jared made it to his side. The mountain rumbled again. They backed away.

"Cottler!" Tellico shouted. "Get away from there!"

The Gray Man did not listen. He knelt beside his silver, picking up a handful of it.

"Cottler!"

But he remained where he was while high above him another cloud of white bulged off the mountainside. Tellico and Jared turned and ran, darting madly along the narrow cliff's edge, deafened by the terrible roar as a new avalanche came down on the old man named Cottler, burying him this time in a grave too deep ever to be escaped.

Tellico and Jared looked at the place where Cottler had been. The wind swirled around the peaks, bitter cold.

"Over at last," Jared said. "Why didn't you just shoot him and be done with it?"

Tellico shook his head. "I don't think I was supposed to kill him. I think I was supposed to salvage what humanity was left in him, if I could."

"You talk like this all was supposed to happen."

Tellico shrugged. "Who can say? Maybe it's like Darius Cottler said—things follow a pattern. It's done now, whatever."

Together they began the long descent to Jerusalem Camp, so battered and weak they could hardly move.

Chapter 22

Spring melted the snow and brought warmth to the Sierras. The meadows bloomed and the air became fresh and warm.

Tellico strode down the hill from his shack and knocked on the door of the Cable house. Anna answered and greeted him.

"Jared in?"

"He's on the hillside again."

Tellico shook his head. "Hard for him to let go. Do you think he'd mind if I joined him there?"

"I don't think he'd mind at all."

Tellico found him beside the new grave that bore the name Isaiah Cable. Jared was seated in a tailor's squat on the ground.

"Jared?"

"Howdy, Tellico."

Tellico squatted beside his friend. "What would Isaiah think of you sitting up here grieving over him day after day?"

"I'm not grieving. I'm saying good-bye."

"He's been dead a month now. It's time for you to make the break."

"That the preacher in you coming out again? What I'm talking about is different. I mean saying good-bye to this valley. The whole town."

Tellico lifted his brows. "That surprises me. I never figured you would leave."

"Maybe I won't. I haven't decided. It's just not the same as before."

"The people?"

"Yeah." Jared plucked a blade of new grass, stood, and began breaking the grass into little pieces as he paced. "He stood up there before them and confessed something the best of them would never reveal if they had been the guilty ones—and they just, well . . . you know how they reacted."

Tellico answered carefully. "They had lost friends and family to a killer who came here because of what Isaiah and the elders did."

Jared tossed down the last fragment of the grass blade. "Yeah. But when it's your own father it hurts mighty bad. I wonder if the response of the people was what killed him."

"Isaiah knew what the price might be when he told the story," Tellico said. "It took a lot of courage. More than Claude had."

Jared nodded. Claude Gregory and Matty had left the valley at the first touch of spring—old people with nowhere to go and no means of support, running from the shame of a thirty-five-year-old sin, told in detail from Isaiah's pulpit. And Claude forever to bear a reminder of that sin in the empty place where once a thumb had been.

"Look yonder—there goes Doc," Jared said. The old man was shuffling across the street toward his undertaking parlor. "I don't see how he does it, bearing the silence and the dark looks. I looked for him to move on, too, but I don't think he's going to."

"Doc's a strong man."

Jared looked at Tellico and smiled. "First time you laid eyes on him you knocked him on his butt."

Tellico chuckled. "Seems a long time ago now. But it's just a season back."

"A long season."

For weeks Tellico and Jared had talked at great length, Tellico revealing more about his own life, his fleeing from the war and the pulpit, and his conviction now growing that he should return to the latter.

"At your old home congregation?" Jared asked.

"Probably not. The man I was then has been too long dead in the eyes of those people. I'm Tellico now, and Tellico I'll stay."

Jared laughed. "A preacher with a false name?"

"Like I said, I'm Tellico now. Nothing false about it."

"You don't have to leave, you know. There's a vacant pulpit in the Jerusalem Camp church."

"That's not for me to fill. But somewhere out there in some little town or on the backside of a mountain there's a place where I'll belong. I think the Almighty will get some use out of me yet."

"So your destiny takes you full circle, right back where you started."

Tellico nodded. "It's like somebody once said to me: You've got to consider there may be a pattern to it all, even if we can't always see it."

Tellico rode out a day later with no good-byes and no glances back.

Jared never left Jerusalem Camp. Time went by and the wounds of the Killing Winter healed.

Witt Essler, who now limped on an avalanche-injured leg, made sure the story of Tellico became part of Jerusalem Camp's folklore. The story grew in the telling until finally Witt believed his own embellishments.

"He was on the run from the law," Witt would say. "He was a gunfighter—I knew it from the beginning. He had that look about him, that bearing and way of holding his hands."

Then he would tell how Tellico had fought the killer in the mountains hand-to-hand until an avalanche buried both of them and only Tellico emerged. On and on, more and more.

Jared corrected the growing myth at first, then gave up. It finally reached the point where his corrections would not have been believed anyway. People wanted to believe Tellico was a gunfighter, so they did.

"He was a preacher, nothing more," Jared told Anna. "Just a war-weary chaplain who ran away from the killing because he couldn't make sense of it all."

Anna slipped her arm around Jared's waist and hugged him. A hawk swooped down from High Ridge over the broad valley, drawing the attention of both.

"Think he'll ever come back?" Anna asked.

"No," Jared said. "But I'm sure glad he came when he did."

ABOUT THE AUTHOR

I was born in 1956 in Tennessee, the state in which I have lived all my life. I wrote my first western at age twenty-two and now I am writing exclusively for Bantam.

My interest in the American West is part of a broader interest in the frontier. I am fascinated by the vast westward expanses on the other side of the Mississippi, but I am equally intrigued by the original American West: the area west of the Appalachians and east of the Mississippi. I hope someday to write fiction set in that older frontier at the time of its settlement, in addition to traditional westerns.

My interest in westerns was sparked in early childhood by television, movies, and books. I love both the fact of the West and the myth of the West; both aspects have a valid place in popular fiction.

I received an undergraduate degree in English and journalism, plus teaching accreditation in English and history, from Tennessee Technological University in 1979. Since that time I have been a newspaper journalist by profession, both as a writer and editor. Today I live near Greeneville, Tennessee, one of the state's most historic towns. Greeneville is the seat of the county that contributed one of America's original frontier heroes to the world—Davy Crockett. Greeneville was also the hometown of President Andrew Johnson and was for several years the capital of the Lost State of Franklin—an eighteenth-century political experiment that came close to achieving statehood.

My home is in rural Greene County. My wife, Rhonda, and I have three children, Matthew and Laura, and Bonnie.